SAVAGE *heart*

Savage Angels MC Series Book Eleven

Kathleen Kelly

Savage Heart
Savage Angels MC Series Book Eleven

Kathleen Kelly

All efforts have been made to ensure the correct grammar and punctuation in the book. If you do find any errors, please e-mail Kathleen Kelly: kathleenkellyauthor@gmail.com Thank you.

ISBN: 978-1-922883-08-7

Edited by Swish Design & Editing
Proofreading by Swish Design & Editing
Book Design by Swish Design & Editing
Cover design by Clarise Tan at CT Cover Creations
Cover Image Copyright
First Edition 2023
Copyright © 2023 Kathleen Kelly
All Rights Reserved

DEDICATION

For SL, who sees me at my worst and my best.
You're the only one I want to be with on this crazy
ride called life.
It's you and me against the world, baby.

SAVAGE
heart

PROLOGUE

LORE MERCER

Standing behind the worn oak bar, my fingers trace the grooves of years gone by as the soft hum of the evening crowd surrounds me. The dimly lit room is bathed in the warm amber glow from the chandeliers which hang around the room. They cast a soft, nostalgic light over the polished counter. The sound of laughter and clinking glasses fills the air, mingling with the heavy notes of the rock band playing in the back of the bar.

God, I love this place.

It's mine and has been for the past five years.

It's my sanctuary, my second home.

The walls are lined with photographs of the ones I love. Some are in celebration, others, like the one

1

of my son and me on his last birthday, bring me joy every time I gaze upon it. Next to it is a picture of Sam Elliott, the actor, who came in one night for a drink.

Although I've owned this bar for five years, I've worked in and around them my whole life. Looking around the room, I take in every detail as I wipe a glass with a towel.

The shrill ring of the old rotary telephone breaks through the comforting noise. Dean, one of my bartenders, walks toward it, but I wave at him, and he goes back to serving his customers.

Slinging the towel over one shoulder, I answer the telephone, "Hello, Rock Anthem Ale House, this is Lore."

The voice on the other end asks, "Hello, my name is Agatha Twist. I'm looking for a Lore Mercer."

"Speaking." I roll my eyes and stare up at the ceiling, thinking she's going to try to sell me something.

"Ms. Mercer, I work at the Baptist Hospital in Pearl County. Ma'am, you're down as the emergency contact for a Tobias Dupont."

My pulse quickens, and my mind races as I imagine the worst. "I'm his mother."

"Ma'am, there's been an accident."

"What happened?" I ask, my voice trembling.

"Ma'am, he's been shot."

A lump forms in my throat as I clutch the

telephone tighter. "How bad?"

"The doctor can tell you more, but, ma'am, I'd hurry to get here."

My legs weaken, and I lean against the bar for support. The room around me blurs, the laughter and clinking glasses now a distant symphony. With a shaking hand, I set the telephone back on its cradle. Taking a deep breath, I collect myself. This is not the place to lose control. The patrons nearest to me at the bar send concerned glances my way. I plaster a fake smile on my face and walk to Dean. He's worked for me for three years and is more than capable of looking after the bar.

"Dean, time to take a break. Walk with me."

I signal for two of the servers to come to the bar.

"What's up, boss?" asks one.

"Dean and I are taking a break. We'll be back in ten." Leaning closer to both of them and lowering my voice, I say, "Don't fuck up."

Dean and I head for my office at the back of the building. I walk in and sit on my desk. Dean locks the door and walks to me, a smirk on his face. His hands land on my hips, and he kisses me.

"I didn't bring you in here for that."

He licks his lips. "I can be quick." Dean kisses my neck as he massages one of my breasts.

Putting a hand on his chest, I push him away. "I need to leave town, and I need you to take care of the place while I'm gone."

The smirk disappears. "Trouble?"

"My son." I swallow hard and shake my head to keep myself together. "He's been shot."

"Jesus, Lore. I'm so sorry."

"Can you feed Cosmo too?"

"Yeah, but you know the fucking cat hates me." He rests his hands on my shoulders. "Take all the time you need. Where are you going?"

Looking into his pretty green eyes, I frown. "The last fucking place I want to go. The one place on this planet I swore I'd never return to."

"Jesus, Lore. Where?"

"Tourmaline, home to the fucking Savage Angels."

CHAPTER 1

LORE

The sun's rays warm me as I sit in my rental car and stare at the Baptist Hospital. It took me a flight and a day's drive to get here. Reporters are everywhere at the front of the entrance, and Savage Angels' members are keeping them all out.

A familiar face walks out of the hospital. He scowls at the mass of people before him, then wanders down the sidewalk, pulling a pack of cigarettes out of his pocket.

Dirt hasn't changed much over the past ten years. He's more weathered, probably from too many biker rallies. His dirty blond hair is touching his shoulders—I guess he's wearing it a little longer. Even from this distance, I can see the scar that goes from his temple into his hair. I always thought it gave him character and, as he's only five foot nine, gave him some street cred. If you're smart, you don't tangle with Dirt. He can more than handle himself in a fight, not with knives or guns, although he's more than capable with these as well. It's his fists you need to watch out for. One punch is normally all it takes for him to have you lying in the dirt with your teeth all over the ground. We have a history, one I walked away from and never wanted to revisit.

With a groan, I open the door to my rental car. Dirt's head swivels in my direction, but I'm sure he knew I was here long before he looked at me. My lips turn down as I stare at him and climb out of the car. He has the hide to give me a chin lift as he takes a drag on his cigarette. Slamming my door, I put my handbag on my shoulder and stalk toward him.

His eyes widen when I pull the cancer-causing stick from his mouth, drop it on the ground, and grind my boot into it.

"Jesus, lady, take a pill."

Removing my shades, I put them on my head. "Those things will kill you, Dirt."

"Lore?" His posture stiffens, and his eyebrows shoot up to his hairline.

"And what the fuck did you and your MC do to my son?"

Dirt stumbles back. "What?"

"Tobias. What the fuck happened to him?"

His mouth drops open. "*You're* Tobias' mother?"

Turning, I give him my back and shout as I walk away, "You always were *quick* on the uptake."

His boots pound heavily on the pavement as he jogs after me. Dirt's hand wraps around my upper arm, and he spins me around.

"You haven't changed at all, have you? Still spitting venom and unkind words at anyone who is in your way." Pointedly, I stare at his hand on my arm, and he lets go. Dirt takes a step back, shaking his head. He sucks in a breath and, in a softer tone, says, "I'm sorry about Tobias. He's a good man."

Never in all the years when we were together did he ever apologize or offer words of comfort. Together, we were toxic, feeding off each other, and eventually, whatever it was I thought we had evaporated. I remember a feeling of relief when it was finally over.

"Can you take me to him?"

Dirt nods, walks ahead of me through the crowd, and straight to the hospital elevators. Once inside, he clears his throat and casts a sideways glance in my direction.

"What?" I ask with a sigh.

"Have you been sacrificing small children?"

Blowing out my cheeks, I reply, "What?"

"It's just you look good, Lore. You haven't aged a day."

His words reignite a familiar feeling, one I

thought was buried in the past. Feigning a cough to mask the smile on the verge of breaking through, I respond with, "Keeping negative people out of my orbit and enjoying life is my secret, *not* sacrificing to the gods."

Dirt chuckles. "Well, whatever you're doing, it's working."

The elevator doors open, and he walks out. My bravado leaves me, and I'm frozen on the spot. Dirt turns around and raises an arm to prevent the doors from closing.

"How bad is he?" I whisper.

Part of me wants to know the truth, but a greater part is terrified I'll lose my son forever.

"Tobias is strong."

"Don't give me that bullshit, Dirt. The one thing you and I did well, maybe too fucking well, was tell each other the truth."

Dirt moves into the elevator and holds out a hand to me. I stare at it, shake my head, and step onto the ICU floor. His lips go together in a hard line, and he gestures toward a waiting room. Without talking, we make our way to it. There's no one else here, and we sit opposite each other. Dirt leans forward, elbows on his knees. His hazel eyes show a depth of emotion I've never seen on him before.

"He took a bullet to the face. His left eye is gone." Dirt licks his lips, and I feel my throat tightening with every word that leaves his lips. "I wish I could tell you he's going to be okay, but Lore, we don't know."

A group of women walk into the waiting room. Most barely have enough clothes on to cover their asses.

One sits next to Dirt. "Thought you went outside for a smoke?"

"I did."

"Where's my coffee?"

Dirt glances at me and says, "Destiny, this is Lore Mercer, Tobias' mother."

A collective gasp sounds in the room as all eyes land on me. Destiny stands and awkwardly throws her arms around my body.

"It's so good to meet you. I'm so sorry I didn't recognize you. Tobias has your picture on his wall at his home."

"You're his girlfriend?" She looks down at her finger with an incredibly large rock on it. "Fiancée?"

"No, no, no, no," Destiny quickly says as she flaps her hands around. "I used to work for Tobias." She looks at the other women. "We all do. I mean, I did. I don't anymore. He's more like family to me. And I'm rambling." Destiny takes a deep breath. "Have you gone in to see him?"

"She just got here, D," replies Dirt.

"Where is he?"

"I'll take you." Dirt stands and holds out his hand.

This time, I put my hand in his and let him guide me away from the waiting area. Together, we pass through a pair of imposing double doors, and immediately before us stands a desk with a nurse engrossed in the contents of a patient chart. Dirt clears his throat to capture her attention, but I step forward, my trembling hands gently resting on the counter's surface.

"My name is Lore Mercer. Tobias Dupont is my son," I softly declare.

She puts down the chart, eyes filled with empathy as she offers a sympathetic nod. "I'll see where the doctor is."

"Can I see him?"

"It's best if you wait to speak to the doctor." Her response is gentle but cautious.

"Look, lady. I'm tired, and I'm scared. I just need to lay eyes on my son. I need to see him. Do you understand?" I urgently plea.

With a quick nod, she says, "Only you." Her eyes flick to Dirt. "You wait here."

Dirt opens his mouth to respond, but I reach out and place a hand on his chest, silencing him. "I'll be fine."

The nurse walks ahead of me down the sterile corridor. Fluorescent lights overhead cast a harsh, clinical glow on the linoleum floors. The rhythmic beep of monitors and the soft murmurs of medical staff in the background create an eerie backdrop to the weighty anticipation hanging in the air. My heart is pounding in my chest as we pass through a maze of rooms filled with patients in various states of critical care. Hushed whispers of hope and despair seem to linger in the hallway, and I feel even more helpless.

The nurse stops near a sink and washes her hands. "It's a sterile environment." She nods toward a gown as she dries her hands on a towel, then drops it into a bin. "Please wash your hands and put on the gown."

I copy her movements, and when we are done, she guides me to where Tobias is. There are four beds, each with a body in them and a nurses' station in front of them.

"Before you touch him, please use the hand sanitizer." She holds her hands under a machine, and gel drips out. "You need to do this every time you visit. Any infection would be catastrophic to him right now."

A shiver runs down my spine as I gaze upon Tobias. Almost on autopilot, I hold my hands under the machine and rub the clear liquid into them. My boy is strong, proud, and full of life.

The body in front of me is motionless, connected to a labyrinth of machines and tubes. His face has a bandage around it, obscuring most of it from me. The tears which have been threatening to fall cascade down my cheeks. Reaching for him, I place his hand in mine, bending to place a kiss on the back of it.

The nurse, her voice soft and reassuring, leans in close and gently explains, "I know all this medical equipment can be overwhelming and frightening, but please remember that your son is in the right place to receive the best care possible. Our team is dedicated to ensuring he gets the attention and treatment he needs to recover."

"*Will* he recover?"

"It's best you talk to the doctor. Let me see if I can find her."

She walks away, leaving me holding on to the only thing I've ever gotten right in my life.

"Jesus, Tobias, what did you get yourself into?" I whisper. There's no flicker of movement, the machines continue to beep, and I feel helpless. "Cosmo says hi. One of the guys from the bar, Dean, is looking after him. You remember Dean, don't you? He's worked for me for a while. He's looking after the bar too. Business is good."

I know I'm rambling, and there's no way to know if Tobias can even hear me, but I feel as though I have to talk to him. To pretend he isn't hooked up to a bunch of machines and looking as though death is waiting to take him.

"Mrs. Mercer?" Turning, a woman in a white coat, wearing glasses, is standing at the foot of the bed. She has a chart in her hands and is reading it.

"I'm Dr. Olivia Grills."

"Yes, that's me. I'm Tobias' mother."

She nods, and her eyes meet mine. She takes a deep breath before she begins, "I just wanted to talk to you about the surgery," her voice is calm and laced with empathy. "We successfully removed the bullet from your son's head. It was a delicate procedure, but everything went as planned. We took every precaution."

I hold my breath, my eyes locked onto hers as I hang on to every word, a glimmer of hope shining through the darkness.

"He's a fighter," Dr. Grills continues, a hint of pride in her tone. "We'll keep monitoring him closely, but I'm optimistic about his chances for a full recovery."

Relief washes over me as I let out a shaky breath. "His eye?"

"Gone." She puts down his chart. "He'll need to wear a prosthetic or a patch. There was nothing we could do to save it."

"Brain damage?"

"I'm optimistic, but we won't know until he wakes up."

Nodding, I look back at Tobias. "And how long will he be hooked up to these machines?"

"It's early days. I'm going to keep him sedated for three more days." I look at her sharply. "It's merely to give him time to heal." Dr. Grills presses her lips

13

together. "The operation went well, but every patient is different. Your son is strong, and we are hopeful there will be no long-standing issues."

"What sort of issues?"

She offers me a smile. "Let's wait and see, shall we?"

Holding onto Tobias' hand, I frown at the doctor. "No, we shan't. Give it to me straight, Doc."

Her eyebrows shoot up, and she says, "Unfortunately until Tobias wakes up, we won't know. He could suffer from headaches. He'll most certainly have to go into physical therapy to learn how to walk and maybe even talk again, but this is all guessing, and I'm not in the business of doing that. Right now, it's a waiting game. When he wakes up, we'll all know the extent of his injuries, but the brain is an extraordinary organ. I've seen people overcome some of the most difficult circumstances. Most take six months to recover, others with physical therapy months or years, but in rare cases, it's as though nothing has happened. It's all up to him." Dr. Grills nods at Tobias. She reaches into her pocket and holds out a card. "This has my numbers on it. If you need to talk to me about Tobias, you call. If I don't answer, leave a message. I could be in surgery or on rounds. Mrs. Mercer, I will call you back, *but* you need to be patient."

"My name is Lore. Please call me Lore." I take the card off her and hold it up. "Thank you."

The doctor nods and walks away.

Staring back down at Tobias, I rub his hand between my own. "Okay, boy, you heard her. It's all up to you. I have no idea how you ended up here, but I can assure you, I'm going to find out. No one messes with my son."

CHAPTER
2

DIRT
Sergeant at Arms, Savage Angels MC

The nurse returns to her post without Lore, and I'm feeling helpless and frustrated at not being able to go with her. I'm not built for waiting. I thrive on direction and purpose, not this agonizing monotony. Waiting around is not what I'm good at. Give me a direction, a purpose, and I'll fill the task, but this monotony of waiting is torture. The nurse gives me the once-over, her eyes landing on my cut.

"She might be awhile. Perhaps you could wait in the waiting room?" she suggests.

"I'm good."

She raises one eyebrow and tilts her head to the side. "I'll word that another way. Sir, please go wait in the visitor's area."

"I only want to make sure she's okay."

"And you can do that from the waiting room."

Not wanting to get kicked out of the hospital, I rap my knuckles on the counter, turn, and push my way through the double doors and back to Destiny. She's in a circle with the other women. They're all holding hands, and it looks as though the strippers are all praying.

When I flop down on a chair, their gathering halts. Destiny approaches me, concern on her pretty face.

"Did you see him?"

"No."

"Did you get an update?"

"No."

Destiny throws her hands in the air. "Jesus, Dirt, what good are you?"

"Were you all praying?"

"Yes." Destiny sits next to me. "Do you know Tobias' mother?"

"Lore and I go way back. She had this spark and drew me in like a moth to a flame, but life has a way of changing things. It's been a decade since I've seen her. We were moving in different directions, and she hated the MC. But the MC is all I've ever known... guess we were doomed from the get-go."

"I've never known you to have just one woman. You seem to go from one to the next," Destiny states.

"Lore was different. Hell, *I* was different. Knew she had a kid but didn't know the kid was Tobias."

Thinking about it, he has her eyes. They're the same shade of deep, moody gray. It's unusual, and when Lore used to get mad, they'd darken like a storm brewing. It was a sure sign she was going to rip me a new one.

"Tobias never told you who his mother was?"

With a shake of my head, I say, "We aren't that close. Maybe he didn't know I knew his mother."

"Do you know Tobias at all? Of course, he knew. That man has more secrets than all of us put together, and he makes a point of knowing everything about everyone around him. He would have known… I'd bet money on it."

"Why wouldn't he have said anything?"

Destiny shrugs up a shoulder. "Maybe because it was over? When he wakes up, you can ask him."

Leaning forward, I pray Tobias does wake up. Lore looked scared shitless getting off the elevator to this floor. The woman I knew was fearless—this Lore is older and maybe a little softer.

"You can all go."

Looking up, Lore is standing in the visitor's area, her gaze sweeping across all of us.

Destiny's hand flies to her mouth, and tears spring to her eyes. "Oh, no! Is he?"

Lore shakes her head, her hair fanning out around her. "No. Tobias is sedated and will be for the next few days. There's no sense in you all being here."

Destiny stands. "We want to be here. We all love Tobias."

Lore nods, but her lips turn down at the corners. "I get that. But as his mother, his guardian, I'm telling you all to leave."

Standing, I confront her. "All due respect, Lore, but you've got no right. Every person in this room is here for Tobias."

Those gray eyes flash darker, and she cocks her head to the side. "Seems to me if it wasn't for *you* people, *my* boy wouldn't be at death's door." Lore flicks her gaze to Destiny. "I'll keep you posted, but for now, I need you all to leave."

Turning, Lore walks away from us without a backward glance. Half the room is crying, and I'm left wondering how I could have thought Lore was softer. She's harder than ever.

"What the actual fuck was that?" asks Destiny as she points at Lore's retreating form.

Holding up both hands, I say, "I'll fix it. Give me a minute."

Striding after Lore, I catch up and spin her around.

"What?" she asks deadpan.

"What?" Lore nods. "For fuck's sake, Lore. All the women in that room care for your son. You can't just kick them all out."

She puts a hand on her hip and juts out the other one. "*Actually*, I can."

"Lore, I get you're going into momma-bear mode, but those women," I point toward the waiting room, then put a hand on my chest. "And the Savage Angels *are* Tobias' family."

"No."

"No?" Frustration colors my tone.

"*No*." Lore leans into my space. "He's my son. I'm listed as his guardian." She flicks a hand. "Those women mean *nothing* to me. Tobias never mentioned them, but the Savage Angels? Yeah." Her lips turn down. "He talked about *all* of you. And if I were a betting woman, I'd bet everything I own it was *because* of the Savage Angels he got shot in the first place."

"Lore—"

"No. No more talking. *You* and *them* can leave. If you don't, I'll have security remove you."

Reaching out, I put a hand on her shoulder. "It doesn't need to be like this. You were once one of us."

Lore shakes my hand off and steps back. "Time doesn't heal all wounds, Dirt."

She turns and walks away, once again giving me her back. This time, I don't pursue her. Instead, I go back to the waiting area to a room full of strippers.

"Lore promised to keep us all informed, but for

the moment, as his mother, she's asked us to keep our distance."

"Us? As in you too?" asks Destiny.

Scowling at the thought of leaving Tobias here without any of us, I reluctantly nod. "She's asked the Savage Angels to vacate the building."

Destiny's eyebrows shoot up, and her mouth drops open. "She asked us *all* to leave?"

Candy steps forward. "But Tobias is family."

The strippers all begin shaking their heads.

Taking a deep breath, I hold up my hands. "Yes, he is. But for now, we need to respect his mother's wishes."

Destiny's lips go into a hard line. "We will." The others begin to argue, so she holds up a finger. "*For now*."

Scowling at me as though it's my fault, the women all file out of the room. I trail after them, but when we get to the elevator, they make it clear I'm not welcome inside.

"Ladies, come on. This isn't *my* fault."

Destiny folds her arms across her chest. "I know a scorned woman when I see one."

Candy nods. "Yep. This *is* your fault."

"I was with Lore *ten years ago*. Hell, I didn't even know she was Tobias' mother."

Destiny quirks an eyebrow at me. "And whose fault is that?"

The doors close, and I'm left staring at their

metallic surface. Cussing, I hit the button repeatedly.

The polished, reflective surfaces of the elevator walls magnify the anxious lines etched on my face. My heart is heavy with the weight of Lore's stern orders, and I can't help but feel a growing sense of frustration. Tobias, although not technically one of us, is our brother and lies in the ICU, sedated and vulnerable. Lore, once one of us, has now cast us aside.

The journey up feels interminable, each floor passing sluggishly, intensifying my unease. My fingers drum an impatient rhythm on the button panel, a futile attempt to hasten its progress.

The elevator doors part, revealing the hushed, pastel-toned surroundings of the maternity ward. The sharp contrast to our world's raw, gritty reality is striking. Babies' cries softly resonate in the air, their lives beginning amidst the antiseptic scent.

Making my way down the corridor, Kade is still at his post. He nods at me and raps his knuckles lightly on the door. It opens slightly, and Dane's dark, intense gaze meets mine. He steps out, and Kade moves to stand next to him.

"Dane," I begin, my voice steady but laced with a hint of trepidation. "We need to talk."

"Trouble?"

"Lore Mercer."

He smiles and shakes his head. "How is the old viper?"

"Venomous."

"She booted us out, didn't she?"

"Yep."

Dane chuckles. "It's your fault you and her ended on such bad terms. Apologize, make it clear we are not leaving Tobias here unprotected."

"Dane—"

He holds up a hand. "Not hearing it. I've got new babies, a wife in the hospital, and two kids at home that I'm sure Bear and Shaz are plying with more sugar than I can handle."

"You mean *they* can handle?" I reply.

Dane shakes his head. "You ever been around kids when they are high on sugar? They're worse than a crack whore going through withdrawal."

Kade barks out a laugh but quickly puts a hand over his mouth when I give him a withering stare. "Is Destiny still here?"

"No, your fiancée left with the strippers, and somehow, it's all my fault."

Dane and Kade exchange a glance and laugh.

"It's not funny."

Dane is six foot seven, a towering presence in any room he enters. As my president, he has my undying loyalty, but right now, laughing at me, I could punch him and feel good about it. It could be my expression, or he's remembering how Lore can be, but he stops laughing.

"I'll talk to her."

"She doesn't want to see us."

Dane grins. "Yeah, she knows I'm not going to abide by *her* orders. Tobias might not wear our colors, but he is our friend. Lore knows this. When Tobias wakes up, if he wants us gone, we're gone. Until then, we protect our own."

"Did you know Lore was his mother?"

The grin disappears, and he nods. "He lived most of his life with his father. Lore has always been a free spirit. She never wanted to be tied down, not even with a kid. Tobias loves her. I think he was grateful she didn't drag him from place to place. Lore had visitation and would see him a few times a year. His father is a good man and never once stopped her from seeing him."

"Why didn't you tell me?"

Dane screws up his nose and looks down at the floor before his gaze meets mine. "Wasn't my place. It was Lore's or Tobias', and neither shared that information with you."

Not sure what to say, I scrub a hand over my face, my fingers tracing the scar that trails into my hairline.

"Go home, Dirt. Sleep on it." He points at Kade. "Go on down to the ICU, remove your cut. We don't need Lore making a fuss."

Kade nods and walks away from us.

"You should have told me."

Dane levels a glare at me. "Go home."

He walks back into the room where Kat and his babies are, shutting the door. Striding back to the elevator, I ride it to the ground floor. There's still some of the MC waiting outside. I point at Zeke, who saunters over to me.

"How's Tobias?"

"No change. I need you to go upstairs and stand guard outside Dane and Kat's room."

"I thought Kade was doing that?"

"Don't make me ask you twice, Zeke."

With a slight nod, he walks past me to the elevators.

Tomorrow, when I'm feeling more charitable, I'll make it up to him, but right now, I don't want to explain to him or anyone how I let a woman get under my damn skin.

CHAPTER
3

DIRT

Thoughts of Lore won't let me sleep. I've tried taking a warm shower, drinking half a bottle of whiskey to drown my thoughts, and even closing my eyes and counting sheep. Yet, here I am, staring at the ceiling and wondering what she's doing.

The night we met, I walked into a bar, and Lore was standing on a table, wearing skintight jeans, a black tank top, and hair down to her ass. She was dancing, singing, and making a spectacle of herself. Her eyes met mine, and when I drew closer to her, she swayed and tumbled backward, leaving me no choice but to catch her as she fell.

Lore laughed, draped an arm around me, and said, "Is your name Catch? Because I've been hooked by your charm."

It was the corniest line I'd ever heard. Lore could always make me laugh. Well, she did in the beginning. Toward the end, all we did was fight.

Over everything.

The club was different back then. We were outlaws, breaking rules, running guns, whores, drugs—anything to make a dollar. Dane has fought hard to get us out of that life, and the MC now feels like a country club. Sure, we still have our fingers in a few illegal activities, but we are slowly becoming dignified. It's no longer a club I recognize. We're in business with the Abruzzi Crime Family, and sometimes I feel like we shouldn't trust them. Not Salvatore Agostino, who's married to Dane's sister, Emily, but the Abruzzis. They don't always play by the rules.

Back then, we were at war with other clubs, and every ride spelled danger. Lore asked me to leave, but I'd fought hard to be Sergeant at Arms, to have a place at the table, and the thought of separating from the only family I'd ever known was unfathomable. The MC was more than just a brotherhood—it was a way of life, and I couldn't abandon it.

It was a sacrifice I was unwilling to make. I loved Lore and still do, but I couldn't leave behind the MC and the camaraderie of my brothers.

Did I make the right decision?

At the time, *yes.*

If I could have kept her, I would have, but Lore wanted out of the MC. It was wild back then. Over the years, I've made decisions with Lore in mind, even though I knew she'd never come back. The house I own is small, but it's on a decent amount of land, and I always hoped she'd return and we could build onto it or simply turn it into a home.

Seeing her brought back all the memories, good and bad, but mostly good. Lore had a wicked sense of humor, and when she loved you, you could tell. She had a way of making you feel like the only man in the room.

Throwing back the sheet, I head for the shower. Sleep isn't coming for me tonight, so I might as well go to the compound and see if anyone is awake. We've got a couple of new prospects, and as a patched-in member, it's my duty to guide and keep them out of trouble.

Yellow tape flickers on the ground near the gate. No doubt the sheriff wanted us to stay out of the clubhouse until he'd finished his investigation, but the only people killed were outside the fence, apart from Tobias, who is still hanging on.

Climbing off my Harley, I stare down at her paintwork. She's a 1958 Duo-Glide with original aqua and white paint work. Kat gave her to me for Christmas one year. She rides like a dream, and I take the best care of her.

There's a light on in the garage, so I navigate the maze of bikes and make my way toward it. It's dimly lit inside, and the air is heavy with the pungent aroma of oil and exhaust. The place hums with activity. A grease-stained Renny is standing beside a workbench with an assortment of scattered tools on it as he stares at a carburetor, perplexed. He leans over it, wrench in hand, with a look of determination on his face.

"Can't sleep?"

Renny jumps and drops the wrench. "For fuck's sake, Dirt, don't sneak up on me."

"Man, I didn't. But you seem focused on the carburetor."

Renny bends and picks up the wrench. "It's out of that old pickup truck, and it's filthy. I'm amazed it was working. I'm going to clean it and then use the compressor to blow all the shit out of it. Why are you here?"

"Couldn't sleep. You?"

He purses his lips, puts down the wrench, and leans against the workbench. "The trouble we had here the other night was all my fault. I'm glad Thea and Zach weren't hurt, but because of me, Tobias was. I'm not sure how to feel about that and what I can do to make up for it."

Surprised at his honesty, I move to stand next to him. "Wasn't your fault. *They* came looking for you, and Tobias was in the wrong spot at the wrong time. It could have been any of us."

Renny scrubs a hand over his face, smearing the grease and giving him a ghoulish appearance. "I'm not sad they are dead. I guess I wish things had turned out differently."

"If wishes were horses, beggars would ride."

Renny cocks his head to the side. "What?"

"It means if wishing could make things happen, everyone would have a Harley, or, in your case, no one would have gotten hurt. What's done is done. We all need to move forward, you included."

Renny nods and stares at his carburetor. "I should get this finished."

"Yeah, I'll be in the clubhouse if you want to get a drink or talk."

Renny screws up his face but nods and goes back to the carburetor. He's been through a lot, so it doesn't surprise me he can't sleep, but taking the blame for the assholes who came after him isn't right.

Leaving the garage behind, I make my way into the clubhouse. The atmosphere shifts as I enter what has always felt like hallowed ground. With low lighting, the scent of well-worn leather and camaraderie in the air, it creates a sense of belonging. The walls are covered with patches and emblems, each telling a story of chapters, adventures, and loyalty.

The heart of the clubhouse is the long wooden bar where a bleary-eyed Rebel is serving drinks. Behind him is an array of motorcycle memorabilia on shelves with bottles of alcohol. There are faded photographs of club members pinned behind it, their expressions a mix of adventure and brotherhood.

A pool table takes center stage, and conversations fill the room, punctuated by laughter. It's a place where allegiances are unbreakable and bonds are formed. Well, it's how I've always felt about the clubhouse. The outside world fades away as I step into a sanctuary of shared experiences and the enduring kinship of those who live for the open road and the unbreakable brotherhood of the club.

"What can I get you, Dirt?"

"Whiskey, straight up." The clubhouse is busier than normal. "Why the crowd?"

Rebel pours my drink. "The gunfire, Tobias, and let's not forget the newest editions to our ranks."

Frowning, I tilt my head to the side. "Who?"

"The twins." Rebel grins. "It's a celebration for them, and also some of the other chapters were worried, so they sent reinforcements."

"And you're telling me this now?"

"Jonas knows. I assumed the VP would tell you."

Shaking my head, I throw back the amber liquid and slam the glass on the bar. "Another."

"You got it." Rebel refills my glass. "Do we know how Tobias is?"

"The doctors have him in a coma. We won't know anything until he wakes up." I lift the glass. "*If* he wakes up."

Rebel jerks his head to the side and steps back from me in surprise. "So he's not out of the woods?"

"Not even close. His mother is at the hospital."

"He doesn't talk about her much. Kinda felt like she wasn't really part of his life."

"Well, she is now." I swirl the whiskey in the glass. "She and I were a thing once."

"Are you Tobias' dad?"

Laughing, I shake my head and sip the drink. "No. She'd already had Tobias by then. Didn't even know she was his mother. Neither of them talked about the other."

"Or you never asked," states Rebel as he moves to serve another member of the MC.

His comment hits a little too close to home. Maybe Rebel is right? I loved Lore, but I didn't really know her, or, more importantly, I only knew the Lore she wanted me to see. The woman I knew wasn't mother material. Sure, we had fun, but I couldn't imagine her being at home cooking and cleaning for a kid.

"Dirt, what brings you out?"

Turning, it's Jonas, the VP of our chapter.

"Can't sleep."

"Dane said you've got woman problems."

Putting the glass to my lips, I drink the rest of the whiskey and say, "Had. It was a long time ago. Haven't seen Lore in ten years."

Jonas frowns. "Lore? I was talking about Destiny and the girls from The Cherry. Who's Lore?"

Sighing, I give him a tight smile. "She's Tobias' mother."

Rebel sidles up to us and says, "They used to be a thing."

Growling at Rebel, I say, "Who the fuck asked you?"

Rebel grins at my anger. "Jesus, Dirt, no need to be so fucking prickly. I didn't know it wasn't common knowledge."

"Well, considering I only *just* told you, maybe you should have."

Rebel's eyebrows shoot up, he winks at Jonas, and moves away from us.

"He's a fucking gossiper."

Jonas sits on a bar stool. "Not defending Reb, but you told him, and you know he can't keep his mouth shut."

"I'm too old for this shit."

Jonas clasps his hands together and puts his

elbows on the bartop. "Bullshit. Do you want to talk about Lore?"

"No." I look at him, and he raises his eyebrows. "How about, *fuck no?*"

"Fair enough." He looks at my empty glass. "How much have you had to drink?"

"Not enough."

"Give me your keys." Jonas holds out his hand.

"Fuck off, Jonas. I could be hammered, and I'd still be fine to ride."

"The cops are looking to crucify us at the moment. If they catch you riding under the influence, they're likely to throw the book at you. Give me your fucking keys," Jonas says with no small amount of authority in his voice.

Reaching into my pocket, I hold out the keys. "No one rides her but me."

"And no one will. Go sleep it off."

As a patched-in member, I have my own room at the clubhouse, but I rarely sleep here. Leaving Jonas, I walk down the hallway and up a set of stairs to my room. Someone has been inside, as fresh sheets are on the bed. Probably one of the club's angels did it for me. Some of those women are looking for anyone in the MC who is high in the hierarchy so they can become old ladies. They're wasting their time with me, but it is nice to have my room cleaned.

Stripping out of my clothes and boots, I fall onto

the bed. Maybe it is the noise from below or the feeling of belonging I get from the clubhouse, or maybe it is all the whiskey I've drunk, but within moments, I'm asleep.

CHAPTER 4

LORE

For three days, I've sat beside Tobias, remembering all the wasted opportunities to spend time with him as a consequence of the decisions I made in my life. Being a mother was never part of the plan. I went to the abortion clinic ready to rid myself of my bump in the road. Tobias' father had other ideas. He really stepped up as the mother and father of our son.

A nurse walks in and picks up his chart, then reaches into her pocket and holds out a sheet of paper.

"What's this?"

"It's a list of hotels in the area. They're all close to the hospital. The first one is a short eight-minute walk."

"You kicking me out?"

She smiles and puts Tobias' chart down. "No, but you need a break." She nods at Tobias. "He's strong and stable, and I hope you don't mind me saying, but *you* need a shower."

Lifting an arm over my head, I smell my arm pit and shrug. "I've smelled worse."

"Right."

Standing, I look down at Tobias. "You've got my number?"

"We do."

"Okay." I hold up the sheet of paper. "I'm going to find a place to shower."

"Get some rest. You're no good to him if you're running on empty."

Not wanting to argue with her, I bend and kiss Tobias on the forehead, then leave the ICU. In the waiting room, Dane Reynolds is talking to a man who looks like a younger version of himself. Dane sees me and stops talking.

"Hey, Lore, you look good."

"Dane."

He smiles at me, and I'm sure, just like in the old days, most of the women in a ten-foot radius would drop their panties and beg for him to notice them.

Not me.

Never me.

His charms didn't work on me then, and they don't work on me now.

I keep walking toward the elevators and hit the button for the ground floor.

"You're leaving?"

"Yep."

"Is Tobias okay?"

"Yep."

"Let me reword this… how is Tobias?"

"Stable."

The elevator doors open, and I step inside.

Dane stands next to me and crosses his massive arms across his equally massive chest. "Come on, Lore, give me something."

Taking a deep breath, I let it out slowly. "We won't know anything until he wakes up. But his left eye is gone, and they shaved my boy's head." My voice breaks, and I step farther into the elevator, putting distance between us.

Dane dips his head to his chest. "I can't imagine what you are going through, Lore. But we're here for you."

With a shake of my head, I look him in the eye. "*I* don't need you. *My son* doesn't need you."

The doors open, and I walk out of the elevator and the hospital.

Camera flashes go off in my face before Dane puts himself in front of me.

"Back off," he bellows at the press. "This lady's son is in the ICU, and she has nothing to do with me."

Puzzled at his declaration, I make a beeline for my rental car. I click the button to unlock it and climb inside. The passenger door opens, and Dane folds his massive form into the car.

"What are you doing?" I snap at Dane, the disbelief still coursing through my veins.

"We didn't finish our conversation," he says, seemingly unfazed by my anger.

"I didn't realize we were having one," I retort, glaring at him.

Dane puts the seat belt on and fastens it. "Well, now you do."

"Get. Out." I growl, my frustration mounting. This is the last thing I need right now. Dane laughs, and I swivel to look at him, anger rising within me. "I'm serious. Get out."

Dane holds up his hands in a gesture of surrender. "No, Lore, we need to talk. If you're looking for the closest hotel to the hospital, take a left as you exit the parking lot."

I scowl, baffled by his sudden helpfulness. "How do you know I'm looking for a hotel?"

Dane looks sheepish, his gaze dropping momentarily. "I paid the nurse to give you the list."

I let out an exasperated sigh. "Great."

Dane tries to get back to the topic at hand. "Lore—"

"No," I interrupt, holding up a hand in his face. "You can't tell me it's not because of you and your

MC that Tobias got shot."

Dane's expression turns serious, and he locks eyes with me. "Actually, I can."

I tilt my head to the side, raising an eyebrow as I stare into his eyes, waiting for an explanation.

Dane takes a deep breath before he explains, his eyes locked onto mine. "Lore, I know this looks bad, and I understand why you might think the MC had something to do with Tobias getting shot, but I swear, it's not like that."

My skepticism hasn't waned, but I let him continue.

"We have a new prospect named Renny. You might have seen him in the news. Renny recently got released from prison for a crime he didn't commit."

"Yeah, but I bet he was guilty of something."

Dane waves a hand in the air. "He's a good guy, but he's been dealt a rough hand. The people who put him in prison came looking for him. It's him they were shooting at, but Tobias was in the crossfire."

I narrow my eyes at him, trying to process what he's saying. "So, you're telling me your MC had nothing to do with what happened to Tobias?"

Dane nods earnestly. "Yes, Lore. Tobias is like a brother to me. I know you know this. We protect our own, and whether you like it or not, Tobias *is* one of *us.*"

My anger starts to wane, but doubts linger. "This Renny is in your MC?"

Dane shrugs. "Yes, but Tobias being shot and the MC having a hand in it are two different things. You've lived the life... you get this." He runs a hand down his face. "I just want to make sure Tobias gets through this, and I want you to feel safe here too."

I chew on my lower lip, torn between anger and concern. "What's your plan, then?"

Dane offers a faint smile, genuine for the first time since our encounter. "Renny is cooperating with the police. He's shared what he knows, and in the meantime, me and my MC will do everything we can to protect you and Tobias."

"Is there still a threat?"

"No, but there's nothing wrong with being cautious."

As I consider his words, I wonder if I've been too quick to judge. Dane might not be the enemy, and if he's telling the truth, we could be allies. But I can't shake the lingering doubts and fears that have taken root in my mind.

"A left, you said?"

Dane nods. "Yep, take a left, drive for a block, then turn right. It's the gaudy blue building."

"Sounds delightful," I reply sarcastically.

"It might look like a smurf threw up, but it's clean, secure, and best of all, it's close to the hospital."

I can't help but chuckle at his choice of words, and the tension between us is momentarily eased.

Despite the circumstances, maybe there's a chance we can work together to get through this ordeal.

CHAPTER
5

DANE
President, Savage Angels MC

The clubhouse is full of unfamiliar faces from different chapters. Jonas has found beds for all of them and fielded questions from Carlos Morales, our local sheriff, about the swell in our numbers. Even though Carlos is a friend, he's made it clear he has no love for the MC. I have no doubt he'll be seeking me out to grill me and make a point of wanting to know the backgrounds of all of them, even though he will have already started the process.

"Dane!" bellows King, the president of the Las Vegas chapter.

"King?"

He engulfs me in a hug, slapping my back

several times.

"How the fuck are you?"

"What are you doing in Tourmaline?"

He leans in, giving me a sideways glance. "What, you're not happy to see me?"

"My home is your home, but King, you're a long way from home."

"Yeah, that's what your VP keeps telling me." He looks outside. "Walk with me?"

King is nearly as tall as me, a little younger, but just as formidable. It's not every day he shows up in Tourmaline—this would be his first visit. We step outside the clubhouse, seeking privacy from those within.

King takes another drag of his cigarette, exhaling a cloud of smoke into the night air. "I've got some business to discuss, something that could impact both our chapters. Sorry about the troubles you've had, but I was already on my way when I heard about the shootings."

I sigh, my shoulders sagging even further. "Yeah, it's a mess. Tobias got shot."

King's gaze turns serious. Tobias is well known in our circles, and King's concern is evident. "Sorry to hear that. How's he doing?"

"He's in the hospital in critical condition," I reply. "The bastards who did it are in the ground."

King nods in understanding. "I get it, brother. We all look out for our own. But keep in mind, the law here doesn't look too kindly on us."

"I know, King. It's a mess, but we weren't the targets, neither was Tobias. Wrong place, wrong time."

He claps a hand on my shoulder, his grip firm. "I'm here because of the Abruzzis."

Confused, I shake my head. "I'm not following."

"They're trying to muscle us out of the casino deals in Vegas. I'm pretty sure all communications in and out of the clubhouse in Vegas are tapped. It's why I'm here in person. Brother, there's a storm coming."

"No."

"So, you haven't heard anything?"

"No," I repeat, my mind racing to catch up with the implications.

"I thought with your connections to Salvatore Agostino, you might be able to shed light on a few things."

"You came all this way?" My surprise is evident.

King exhales a stream of smoke and offers a grim smile. "When it comes to protecting our territory, Dane, we do what we must. We've got to weather this storm together."

As King and I stand in the dusty parking lot, my mind is a whirlwind of thoughts and questions. Salvatore, my brother-in-law, is a man of influence and connections within the Abruzzi Crime Family. If there were a problem, he'd surely have been in the know, but I haven't heard a word from him.

"Have you told anyone about this?" I ask, my brow furrowing.

King shakes his head solemnly. "No. I've got a rat in my house, Dane, and I'm not sure who I can trust. How about you? Do you trust everyone here?"

I glance over at the clubhouse, my gaze scanning the various members from different chapters who have been coming and going since the event. "Following the shooting, we've had members from different chapters in and out of our clubhouse, but I'm confident those closest to me are trustworthy."

King casts a critical eye around our compound. "You've got a nice little setup here. It's different from Vegas."

"It's a small country town," I explain. "There's no glitz or glamor. What you see is what you get."

He drops his cigarette on the ground and grinds it out with his heel. "Yeah. Let's find a spot to sit and talk, and I'll tell you what I know."

"To be on the safe side..." I suggest. "I'll have Rebel sweep for bugs before we sit down. Until then, are you hungry? Can I buy you a meal?"

King grins, the tension of our conversation momentarily easing. "Fuck, yeah."

Turning, King and I both walk back into the clubhouse. Rebel is leaning over Ruby, his woman, attempting to teach her how to set up a shot for a game of pool. From my perspective, it looks like he's trying to screw her over the pool table.

"Rebel, got a minute?" I call out to him.

He straightens, adjusting himself as he does, and walks toward me. "Yeah, Prez?"

"Can you give the chapel a sweep?" I ask. "After it's done, no one goes in or out, even if they are patched in."

"No one?" Rebel seeks clarification.

"No one until King and I return," I affirm.

"You got it."

Rebel heads down the hallway to retrieve our surveillance equipment, and I turn to King.

"There's a diner in town. It's got good food. Come on, it's on me," I offer.

"Great, I'm starved," King replies, extending his hand toward me. "I forgot... congratulations on the birth of your twins."

I grasp his hand firmly. "Yeah, two boys, Blaze and Gunner. My woman did good."

King nods and walks outside. When I keep going past the line of Harleys, he stops and crosses his arms.

"What?" I ask.

"You're not riding in?"

"Man, it's a ten-minute walk, even at a stroll. The exercise will do you good."

King tilts his head to the side and gives me the once-over. "Walk?" He says it like it's a dirty word.

"Yep," I reply with a hearty chuckle before moving on.

It's not long before he falls into step beside me.

"Why walk when you have a bike?"

"Exercise."

King grunts, and we walk in silence until we get to the café. I open the door for him, and he walks ahead of me.

Thea is behind the counter and smiles warmly at me. "Hey, Dane, good to see you."

"Thea," I say, gesturing toward King. "This is King, visiting from Vegas."

"Nice to meet you. Sit wherever you want. It's been a slow day."

Smiling at her, I sit in the booth at the window, and King slides in across from me.

"She's cute."

"She's taken."

He sighs and picks up a menu.

"Thought you had a woman?"

"Had. Didn't work out. They are too much work."

Chuckling, I say, "They are if you pick the wrong one."

King's lips turn down at the sides, and he shrugs. "What's good?"

"Everything. But the fried chicken will change your world."

King grins, a touch of skepticism in his expression. "Man, that's a big claim. I'm from

Vegas… we're a melting pot with a world of flavors."

Nodding, I say, "Yeah, but trust me."

King puts down the menu. "With my life, brother."

Thea sidles up to our table. "You want your regular, Dane?"

"Yes, please, Thea."

She acknowledges me and then turns her attention to King. "And for you?"

"Fried chicken."

"You want whipped potatoes with that?"

"Yeah, with gravy and green beans."

"Great. Drinks for you both?"

"Coffee," we both chime in simultaneously.

Thea grins. "You boys are all the same."

King leans back in the seat, extending his arm across the top of it. "You're a regular boy next door, aren't you?"

"What do you mean?"

He waves a hand in the air. "Small town, you know everyone… wife, kids, and I bet you even donate to the local high school. Am I right?"

Frowning, I ask, "Your point?"

King leans forward and clasps his hands together on top of the table. "It's been quite a while since you've been in the fight. Hell, when was the last time you went on a pack ride, joined a rally, or got your hands dirty? Maybe you've become so accustomed to this lifestyle you've forgotten what

49

it's like to roll up your sleeves and get down and dirty in the trenches?"

I smile at King, and whatever he sees, he moves away from me. Sucking in a deep breath, I let it out slowly. Peering into his eyes, I don't speak until he shifts slightly, indicating his discomfort.

"You got voted into your presidency."

"So did you," he fires back.

"Yeah, but not until it got messy," I respond, my voice firm. "Not until I had to battle for my seat at the table. I thought you were savvy, King. The old ways are fading, and we've got to adapt, but if you think for one moment I won't take whatever measures necessary to safeguard what's rightfully mine, well, you'd be a fool."

Thea arrives at the table, puts a cup in front of each of us, and pours coffee into them. "Food isn't far away. Howie said to ask if you want to take pie home to Kat?"

King smirks. "Yep, you're a regular hard-ass."

Thea leans down and looks King in the eyes. "Yes, he is." King's gaze shifts to her. "When the bullets were flying, Dane was down in the thick of it, helping rescue Tobias. Bullets were literally flying. I don't know who you are, but you'd best watch your tone." Thea looks at me, nods, and struts away.

"You sure she's taken?"

Ignoring the question, I ask, "Are you here to talk

business, or are you here to fuck with my chapter?"

King holds up his hands. "Business." He shakes his head. "Sorry. I was out of line."

"Yes, you fucking were."

He lowers one hand, holding it to his chest, and waves the other in the air. "I apologize. If it wasn't for you and your forward-thinking, the Savage Angels would not be in the position of power they now are. But I'm telling you, we're being muscled out."

"Not here."

"Dane—"

"Not. Here." Casting a cautious glance around the café to see if anyone is listening, I lower my voice and say, "We don't shit where we eat. This is our town. We look after those in it, and yes, we donate money to the local high school and clinic. A wise man once told me public perception is the most important thing, and you have to be able to spin anything."

Which isn't entirely true. The saying is, 'Public perception is the most important thing, and Dave can spin anything.' Dave is Kat's manager and surrogate father. He keeps The Grinders, Kat's band, in the public eye with just the right amount of rock 'n' roll edge to make them relevant but clean enough that mothers' groups don't picket their concerts.

"Spin?"

With an exaggerated sigh, I respond, "You know what it's like being the president. Some days it's a breeze, and others, it's like trying to herd cats. There are power struggles, conflicts, and most notably, other patched-in members attempting to dictate how to run things."

Recognizing that I'm referencing him, King nods. "I meant no disrespect."

"Yeah, you did," I retort. "Do it again, and I'll send Thea after you." My voice carries a stern tone, and he takes a moment to process my words.

He smiles and playfully wags a finger at me. "You're messing with me."

"Yes, and no. It won't be Thea." I lean in closer to him. "It'll be me."

Thea returns with our food and puts a plate in front of each of us. "You good, Dane?"

King chuckles. "What, are you going to give me a good talking to?"

"No," she replies. "I'll call Judge, and you'll vanish, never to be seen again because *that's* how we operate." Thea sets the cutlery in front of King. "Enjoy your meal."

"You let women talk to brothers like that?"

"Just the ones who can take care of themselves."

We eat in silence, and Thea gives King the cold shoulder whenever she comes to our table to refill coffee. For a woman who could barely look me in the eye when she first moved here, she seems to have decided the Savage Angels are good people. Well, the ones in Tourmaline, at least.

The door to the café opens, and Judge stands at our table.

"Hey, Prez. Rebel did a sweep of the clubhouse, not just the chapel. Everything came up clean."

"Judge, have you met King? He's the president of the Las Vegas chapter."

Judge holds out his hand. "No, I haven't. Welcome to Tourmaline, *home* of the Savage Angels."

King shakes his hand. "The mother chapter."

"You better believe it." Judge releases his hand, nods at me, and leaves the café.

Howie walks over and hands me a box tied with string. "For Kat. Tell her I said hello, and I hope we see her soon."

"Thanks, Howie, and I'll pass it along."

Howie smiles, gives me a nod, and then walks back behind the counter.

Looking at King, I ask, "You finished?"

The only thing left on King's plate is some potato and chicken bones.

"It was good. You were right."

Standing, I throw some bills on the table. "I always am, *brother.*"

Sitting around the table in the room we hold church, I wait for the men to introduce themselves. King came with his VP and another member of his chapter.

"Okay, we're all family here. King, tell us what you *think* you know."

His lips go into a hard, thin line as he stares at me, and then he nods and says, "Yeah, I deserved that. I disrespected you in your house, and I shouldn't have. I apologize, but I'm under a lot of pressure to get this sorted."

I acknowledge his statement with a nod of my head. It's important in our world to address these matters with honesty and directness. King's willingness to admit his wrongdoing is a positive sign.

"Respect within our family is crucial. Let's move forward and focus on the business at hand. We're all ears."

King takes a deep breath, visibly relieved. "We've been hearing rumors about a rival gang encroaching on our territory. Word on the street is that they've been making moves and trying to take control of the drug trade in our area. Their leader is known as 'Shadow,' and he's been recruiting aggressively. They have backing from someone with money, and the Abruzzi family has slowly been weeding us out of the casinos." King leans back in the chair. "And some of our members have gone missing. At first, we didn't notice. A couple were nomads, and one had a drug problem, but it happened over a period of time. We are now up to fifteen members missing."

"Did you report them as missing to the police?" asks Jonas.

"Some, not all. But the cops don't care. You know how they see us."

Jonas is a seasoned member of our MC. He frowns, then says, "It's not the first time we've had rival gangs looking to encroach on our turf, but this 'Shadow' character seems to be more organized and ambitious. If the Abruzzis are supporting him, what's their end game? To wipe us out or push us out?"

Dirt says, "I've been hearing similar rumblings with the Chicago chapter. It's home base for the Abruzzis." His gaze comes to me. "It's better to address this now before it becomes a full-blown turf war."

I nod in agreement, then turn back to King. "We need to protect our territory. We'll gather more intelligence and devise a plan to deal with this threat. The MC has numbers on our side, and we've worked hard to get where we are... that's our strength. The Abruzzis don't know what we can do, but I'm happy to show them."

King nods in agreement, clearly relieved we're taking the threat seriously. "What more intelligence do you need?"

"Salvatore Agostino is my brother-in-law. If something is going down with the Abruzzis, he'll know."

King squints at me. "But he hasn't come to you before now, so what makes you think he'll help us? This has been happening for months. Everyone knows Salvatore Agostino is a cold killer who wants the Abruzzi crown. He's in so tight with those people, he can't be trusted."

"It's true Sal wants to lead the Abruzzi Crime Family. He's been open about his aspirations. But King, Sal *is* family."

At my words, he widens his eyes. I've just vouched for Sal, which means if he is turning a blind eye to the problems in Vegas and hasn't warned us, I'm as good as dead.

Hours later, I find myself at home with Blaze

cradled in my arms, lying next to Kat as she nurses Gunner. The soft glow of the television flickers in the background, casting a warm, dim light across the room.

"You're quiet," Kat observes, her voice hushed and gentle.

"Sorry, darlin'. Club business," I reply, my gaze drifting from our newborn son to Kat, who wears a concerned expression.

"A problem shared and all that," Kat suggests, reaching for the remote to turn off the television.

I look down at Gunner and say, "You've got enough to worry about."

Kat reaches over and pats my leg. "If that's your way of saying it's none of my business, that's okay. But if you want to talk to someone independent of the conversation, I'm your girl."

I chuckle. "Yes, you are. We don't have secrets. There's been some pushback in Vegas and Chicago. Members from both chapters are missing. I've been so wrapped up in you and our family that I may have dropped the ball."

"Did either of the chapter presidents reach out to you?" Kat inquires, her eyes filled with concern.

"No," I reply, shaking my head. "And I rang Sal today, but he hasn't called me back."

Kat tilts her head to the side, her brow furrowing slightly. "So, no one told you they were having problems? Sal would have called if he knew something was up, but you're supposed to be a mind reader and just know if there's an issue?"

She's right, and her words hit home. If the other chapters don't communicate with us, I have no way of knowing what's happening. With the recent shooting in Tourmaline, I asked Rebel to inform the other chapters about the situation, which is why so many members came to town.

"Have I told you how much I love and adore you?" I say, attempting to lighten the mood.

Kat raises her eyebrows in surprise. "Not in a while."

"I love you," I affirm, grinning at her.

She tilts her head the other way, a mischievous glint in her eyes. "You're missing some information."

"I adore you," I add, laughing.

Kat reciprocates with a smile. "That's it. Now, put Blaze down and go ring Sal. He's on our side. There's no way he'd betray you."

Leaning in, I kiss her lips before standing and gently placing Blaze in his crib. I look down at Kat and ask, "Come on, darlin', give him up."

Kat kisses Gunner on the forehead before letting me take him from her arms. "Okay. I'll just take a ten-minute nap."

The twins are wrapped in matching white blankets adorned with little blue guitars.

"When's Dave coming?"

Kat glances at the clock. "Didn't I tell you?"

"No."

"They'll *all* be here by the end of the week."

By 'all' she means her band members in The Grinders will arrive too. A house full of people is on the horizon, and I can't help but wonder how that will affect the dynamics.

"Will that make you happy?" I ask.

Kat's smile is radiant. "Having them all here makes me happy, but I'm already happy with you and the twins... both sets."

I bend down and kiss her softly on the lips. "Sleep. I'll take a baby monitor with me, so if they stir, I'll hear them."

I go downstairs to the kitchen at the back of the house. Dirt is sitting at the dinner table, sipping what appears to be coffee.

"Hey, brother, what brings you out here?" I greet him.

Dirt smiles at me. "Wanted to talk to you but didn't want to interrupt family time. I figured sooner or later you'd come down for caffeine or something stronger."

"You made a pot of coffee?" I ask, noting the pot on the warmer.

"Yeah," Dirt replies. "It's been one of those days."

I grab a mug from a cupboard, fill it, and sit across from him. "It sure has."

"How are Kat and the kids?"

"All good. What have you learned?" I ask, wanting to get straight to the point.

"Guru thinks the money from the casinos isn't adding up. I need to look into it, but it seems like King hasn't kept an eye on things, and it's short."

Sipping my coffee, I lean back in my chair, contemplating the gravity of the situation. "And the missing members?"

Dirt's expression darkens. "That's a real thing. Chicago, Vegas, and New Jersey are missing members. I'm waiting on the others to come back to us."

I can't help but express my frustration. "Why didn't anyone check in? Why are we only finding out about this now?"

Dirt shrugs. "It's not easy for all the chapters to go straight. You heard King say the new MC muscling in is stealing his drug trade. I'd bet my last dollar that's the real reason he came. Everyone knows you and Sal are tight. If he could discredit you, get you out, or worse, it paves the way for him to take over."

I scoff at the notion. "Like fuck it does."

Dirt raises his hands in a conciliatory gesture. "I'm not saying I want that to happen, but he's come a long way to tell you something he could have communicated through the proper channels. The man disrespected you, and you did a dumb thing, my friend, by calling Sal family."

"Sal *is* family."

"I know," Dirt acknowledges. "But you saying that in front of outsiders isn't good. Have you spoken to Sal?"

"I'm waiting for him to ring me back."

Dirt shakes his head and takes a contemplative sip of his coffee. "Not good."

My cell phone rings and I look at the screen. It reads *brother-in-law*.

I hold it up for Dirt to see. "Here he is now." I slide my finger across the screen to answer the call. "Sal, how are you?"

"Good, Dane. Is Kat okay?"

"Yes, Kat and the twins are fine."

He sighs. "Thank the gods. I was worried. What can I do you for?"

"Sal, we need to have a sit-down."

"Problem?"

"Yeah."

"Hang on."

There are muffled voices in the background, and after a moment, he comes back on the line. "We'll be there tomorrow."

"We?"

"Emily and the children want to visit and meet the newest editions of our family."

Resting a hand on the back of my neck, I say, "Now might not be the best time. There are lots of outsiders in town."

"Are you saying we're not welcome?"

"No," I reply quickly. "Dave is coming in with Luther, and the band is coming in from all over."

"We could stay at the motel in town, or you could rent us a cabin."

"You're family... you'll stay with us. We have the room, but bring Tony with you."

Tony is Sal's personal bodyguard. He never goes anywhere without him, and me telling him to bring him should signal there is trouble in Tourmaline.

"I understand. We'll leave as soon as we can."

"Good."

"Dane, should I be worried?"

Not wanting to say too much over an unsecured line, I say, "Safety in numbers."

"Family will always look after family."

"Yes, brother, love and loyalty."

"See you tomorrow." Sal ends the call.

"Well, that sounded as cryptic as fuck," observes Dirt.

Putting the cell phone on the table, I say, "Yeah, needed him to know he might be walking into something and to bring more muscle, but also to let him know I will do my best to look after them."

"Of course you will. Emily is your sister."

"It's not just Emily. There are the kids and Sal. Can you imagine the backlash if Sal was hurt by one of us here? It's exactly what the Abruzzis would need to turn against us."

"If money is going missing from the casinos, that's Sal's deal. He's the one responsible."

Frowning at Dirt's implications, I slowly shake my head. "No way would Sal undercut us."

"I hope not."

Not wanting to discuss this any further tonight, I change the subject. "Do we know how Tobias is doing?"

Dirt picks up his coffee cup. "I need a refill. What about you?" He stands and walks over to the coffee pot.

"Nice deflect."

"The nurses say there's no change. He comes out of the coma tomorrow."

"And Lore?"

Dirt looks pained as he retakes his seat at the table. "She fucking hates me."

"There's a fine line between hate and love."

He takes a sip of coffee and winces as though it tastes bad. "No, it's hate. I'm going to try to speak to her again tomorrow, but so far, she's given me the frozen shoulder."

"Not just cold, hey?"

He shakes his head. "Nope, hell has definitely frozen over."

"I spoke to her. Lore is in full momma-bear mode. I made her understand what happened to Tobias wasn't on us."

"Wasn't it, though? If he hadn't come to the

party, if we hadn't let Renny join, well, maybe none of this would have happened."

"There's a lot of what-ifs in there, Dirt. Don't let Lore get in your head and twist things. You aren't the same man you were. Hell, it's been ten years… we've all changed. Besides, Tobias is no angel. There are a few skeletons in his closet."

"Are you saying it's *his* fault?"

Throwing my hands in the air in frustration, I say, "No, of course not. I'm saying we've all changed, but you letting Lore tell you it's your fault or the club's fault is wrong."

Dirt's fingers lightly drum on the coffee cup. "You're right, brother. I can't let Lore get into my head. We've all evolved, and Tobias isn't without his own issues. This isn't the club's fault."

I am glad to see he's not internalizing all the blame. "We have to stand together and face the challenges head-on."

Dirt takes another sip of his coffee. "Well, I hope I can get through to her and make her see we're not devils in disguise."

I offer a sympathetic smile. "Lore is a strong-willed woman, and she's fiercely protective of her family. I think it's that very quality that drew you to her in the first place."

He chuckles softly. "Yeah, she's always been a force to be reckoned with."

I lean forward, resting my elbows on the table.

"Keep trying, Dirt. Sometimes, it takes time and patience to mend fences. You two have a lot of history, and not all of it was good."

Dirt nods then shifts the conversation. "Speaking of family, what do you need me to do for Sal's visit?"

I glance at my cell phone, still sitting on the table, a reminder of the impending family gathering. "Get Rebel to sweep my house and find six members you trust to keep an eye on things while everyone is here."

"Who else is coming in?"

"Dave and the band... all of them and their partners."

Dirt smirks. "Family will always look after family, right?"

I return his smirk. "You got it. Love and loyalty."

With our unspoken agreement to focus on those closest to us, we finish our coffee in contemplative silence.

There are challenges ahead with the missing members and potential financial issues in the casinos, but we'll face them as a united front.

CHAPTER
6

DIRT

The hospital lobby is a cavernous expanse of white linoleum and sterile fluorescent lights, but it's not the clinical cleanliness that strikes me as I stride through its automatic sliding doors. It's the sensation of a foreign territory and antiseptic air. I may be out of my element, but I'm on a mission to talk to Lore and see if Tobias is awake.

The guard, a burly man with biceps like tree trunks, meets me with a wary look. I can feel his eyes studying me, taking in the tattoos that snake up my arms and the scars that crisscross my hands. I'm not surprised. It's not every day a guy like me walks into a place like this.

"Can I help you, sir?" he asks, his voice hesitant, his hand inching toward a radio on his belt.

I tilt my head, meeting his gaze with eyes unwavering. "I'm here to see a friend," I reply, my voice low and gravelly.

The guard's fingers twitch, but he doesn't reach for his radio. He knows who I am. Hell, everyone who lives near Tourmaline or Pearl knows who the Savage Angels are.

"The elevators are that way," the guard mutters, his eyes darting around as if afraid someone might catch him talking to a guy like me.

He has to know I've been in and out of this hospital and know where the elevators are located. But I point in the direction of them and give him a chin lift. He nods and walks away from me, his hand resting on his belt. I suppose he thinks he's done his due diligence by talking to me. The man probably thinks he's the big man on the hospital grounds.

Entering the elevator, I hit the button for Tobia's floor. When the doors open, I check in with Zeke, sitting in the waiting room.

"Hey, Dirt."

"Zeke." I offer by way of a greeting. "How's it going?"

"Either I'm alone in here, or it's filled with grieving relatives. How long do I have to babysit Tobias?"

"Until Dane tells us not to." Zeke rolls his eyes. "Any news on Lore?"

"You mean Tobias?"

Scowling at him, I cross my arm over my chest.

"She just got back. They're taking him off the sedatives today."

"I thought that was supposed to happen a day or two ago?"

Zeke shrugs. "All I know is it's today."

I give him a two-fingered wave and head toward Tobias' room. The nurse on duty, a wife of one of our members, nods at me as I pass the nurses' station. Standing at a basin, I quickly wash my hands and dry them according to the laminated directions on the wall, then put on a gown.

I don't know what I expect when I enter that room, but the sight before me still hits me like a punch in the gut. Tobias lies pale and still with tubes snaking in and out of his body, a lifeline to a world that's slipping away.

Lore is nowhere to be seen, so I move a chair next to the bed, my knees creaking as I sit down. Looking at him, my throat constricts. There's a peacefulness about him, an air of surrender as if he's battling something far bigger than he ever did in life. Sitting here, I watch my friend fight for his life, surrounded by the sterile world that is so far removed from the chaos we once embraced. Tobias was never a patched-in member of the MC, but his loyalty ran as deep as any ink on leather. He's our silent partner in this sordid world, the man who has made more than one strip club flourish under the flickering neon lights.

Tobias is good with women—not in a lecherous way, but in a way that they trust him, no questions asked. He can see beyond the allure of the stage and the flicker of dollar bills, delving into the dancers' psyche, understanding their hopes, dreams, and vulnerabilities. It's a rare skill that makes him indispensable in a business that thrives on the fringes of society.

Take Destiny, for instance. She was just another face in a sea of sequins and stilettos, a girl with dreams, just like the rest of them. But Tobias had a way of connecting and peeling back the layers of ambition and insecurity. He found out what made her tick and fueled her fire. In turn, she became the club's star attraction who could command the attention of every man in the room with a single sultry sway of her hips. She was a success story, and Tobias was the mastermind behind it all. He guided her to law school, and as his headline act, she made it through without a huge debt over her head—something most of her peers never achieved.

But success in our world is always a double-edged sword. Destiny, despite her newfound fame and confidence with study, was still vulnerable. And when she was attacked, it was Tobias who stepped in, ready to protect one of his own. He didn't need a patch on his back to be a brother.

In a world where the pursuit of pleasure can

often overshadow any sense of purpose, Tobias has a knack for finding those rare gems who will work hard for us. He sees something in them, something more profound, a yearning for a life that extends beyond the confines of the strip club. He nurtures their dreams and guides their ambitions, and in return, they will give their all for the club.

Even those who eventually move on to bigger and better things, who leave behind the dimly lit stage, still reach out to Tobias. They're still connected and willing to lend a hand when the MC needs it because they know Tobias is a man who never forgets his friends.

In the shadowy world of strip joints and motorcycle clubs, Tobias is a unique force, a silent protector, and a mentor to those who dare to dream beyond the neon lights. He's the key that unlocks the potential of every woman who crosses his path.

I've often wondered why he never settled down. There was a woman, once, long ago. She came when he called after Destiny was hurt. Pulling out my phone, I go through my contacts until I find Mel's number. I hit call and hold the phone to my ear.

"Hello, this is Melody Carter."

"Mel? It's Dirt."

"From Tourmaline? The Savage Angels, Dirt?"

"The one and the same."

"Is Destiny okay?"

"It's not Destiny I'm calling about, it's Tobias."

There's a sharp intake of breath. "He's the man who got shot. Is he the survivor or one of the dead?"

"Survivor. He's in the Baptist Hospital in Pearl." She doesn't speak. "Mel, are you there?"

"Yes. I'm coming."

The line goes dead, and I stare down at the screen. A pair of boots comes into view. Looking up, Lore is staring down at me.

"Tell me you didn't just phone *Tobias* Mel."

"Seems like I don't need to tell you."

Lore puts her hands on her hips and stares up at the ceiling. "Jesus, Dirt."

"I thought she should know. They seemed close."

Her head falls forward, and she sighs. "They were until *she* left *him*." Lore spins on her heel, giving me her back. "Jesus, Dirt, what makes you think he'd want to see her?"

Standing, I lay a hand on her shoulder. "He might not want to, Lore, but maybe people need to see him."

Lore shrugs my hand off and turns around. "He's *my* son."

"He is, Lore, and this is going to come out all wrong, but none of his friends know about you. I've fielded phone calls from lots of folks who want to see him or know how he's doing, but you seem determined to keep us all away."

Lore waves a hand at me. "And clearly, with you being here, that's working."

Keeping my hands at my sides for fear I might choke the life out of her, I say, "You trying to be the best mom in the world by keeping his friends at arm's length isn't going to sit well with Tobias when he wakes up."

She steps back as though I've slapped her.

"Lore, I know you're angry, and if it makes it any easier for you, I'll keep away. But Tobias has a family here. He has friends and a life, one you don't know anything about."

Her gaze drops to the floor, and her nostrils flare a little as she takes deep breaths. The room feels heavy with unspoken tension as if it could shatter at any moment.

With a sigh, she finally lifts her eyes to meet mine. They're filled with a mixture of sorrow and frustration.

"You don't understand, Dirt," she says, her voice trembling. "I've spent years believing I was doing what was best for him. I kept away and let his dad raise him. At the time, I believed I was doing right by Tobias, but I wasted all that time. You're right. I don't know my son, at least not as well as I should or would like to. If he dies—"

I step closer. "Lore, we're all here for you and him."

She nods slowly, her tears shimmering in her eyes. "I know I've made mistakes. But I can't lose him, not now, not after all these years."

My heart aches for her, understanding the depth of her pain. I reach out and gently place a hand on her shoulder. "Lore, don't talk like that." I glance down at Tobias. "He's still here."

Lore looks at me with a mixture of gratitude and fear. She nods and steps back, and my hand falls to my side as she once again puts space between us.

"He's breathing on his own. The doctor seems happy with his progress, but he won't wake up." A single tear falls down her cheek, and she quickly brushes it away. "I'll let one person in for ten minutes at a time during visiting hours."

"Thank you." Lore acknowledges me with a quick chin lift. "Can I get you anything?"

"No, I'm good." She moves around the bed and sits down.

"Do you mind if I stay for a while?"

"No." Lore picks up Tobias' hand and rubs circles on it with her thumb as she stares at his face.

Sitting and doing nothing is not something I can do. Lore seems content to stare at Tobias and say nothing.

After a while, I clear my voice and lean forward, elbows on my knees. "Where are you living now, Lore?"

She looks at me out of the corner of her eye. Her expression shrouded in a mix of amusement and curiosity. "Willowbrook Falls."

I raise an eyebrow, my curiosity piqued. "Never

figured you for a small town."

Lore shifts in her chair, her gaze now locked onto mine, but she never releases her grip on Tobias' hand. "It's bigger than Tourmaline and Pearl."

"I've ridden through it," I reply, recalling the quaint streets and the picturesque landscapes I'd seen during my brief visits.

She leans forward, her eyes glinting with a hint of mischief. "I own a bar."

I can't help but smile, genuinely surprised. "Really?"

Lore frowns, perhaps detecting a hint of skepticism in my tone. "Yes. Why is that so hard to believe?"

Waving a hand dismissively, I say, "No, you misunderstand me. You've always had a good head for business, but I guess I never thought you'd own a bar." Lore tilts her head to the side, studying me intently. "The life is hard."

"In what way?" she asks.

Chuckling, I shake my head. "You've always been good with people. But a bar is filled with people and alcohol that can either turn them into devils or angels."

Lore's eyes light up as she talks about her business. "A bar is easy. They come in for drinks, and I serve them with a side of great music, good employees, and tasty bar food." Her passion for her work is evident in her animated expression. "It's open seven days a week, but thanks to good staff, I only work five."

Curious, I ask, "Is it hard to get good workers?"

Lore rolls her eyes, a hint of exasperation in her voice. "Oh, yes. They either skim from the register, give out free drinks to all their friends, or just don't show up for their shift."

Even though she's complaining, there's a genuine smile on her face, revealing her love for the challenges and rewards of her chosen career.

"How long have you owned it?"

"Five years. It's called Rock Anthem Ale House."

"Cool name," I remark.

"Yeah." Her voice softens, and she looks back to Tobias. "He helped me pick the name."

Standing, I clear my voice. "Well, I've taken up enough of your time. Call me when he wakes up."

Lore stands, letting go of Tobias' hand. "Thanks for coming and checking in."

Not sure what to say, I nod at Lore, offering an awkward two-fingered wave before I head for the elevators, my mind still racing with the conversation. Standing in front of the elevators, I practically punch the button to take me to the lobby, the annoyance at myself for not being able to speak to Lore rising to the surface.

Zeke's voice breaks through my thoughts. "Went that well, did it?"

I sigh, not in the mood for small talk. "Yeah," I

mutter, pushing the elevator button again as if the sheer force of my frustration could make it arrive faster.

Zeke presses on, concern etched in his voice. "How's Tobias?"

"Stable, but he's not awake," I reply, my tone tinged with exhaustion and anxiety.

Zeke's next question hangs in the air. "Is that good or bad?"

"Fucked if I know," I snap, my frustration boiling over. I run my hands through my hair repeatedly, trying to alleviate some of the tension. "But he's strong. He's a fucking powerhouse, and there's no fucking way that man is going to die from one lousy bullet. I've been shot, stabbed, and worked over, and *I'm* still here. Tobias is *going* to be fine," I grit out angrily, hitting the elevator button again and again as if my repeated presses could somehow change the situation.

Zeke's concern deepens, and he addresses me with a hint of worry in his voice. "Ah, Dirt, are you okay?"

The doors finally open, and I don't answer him. I stalk inside, turn around, and notice Lore standing behind Zeke. She walks past him and joins me in the elevator. The doors close, and she moves to stand in front of me, her hands gently resting on my upper arms.

"Thank you," she says, her voice soft and filled

with emotion.

I meet her gaze. Surprise and gratitude overwhelm me. "What for?"

Lore swallows, her eyes searching mine. "For not giving up on my son."

Her words hit me like a wrecking ball, and I find myself unable to speak. But the look in her eyes tells me that this is the beginning of something, a fragile bridge between past grievances and an uncertain future.

Sucking in a deep breath, I finally muster the words I've been struggling to find, my voice barely a whisper, "Lore, I—"

But before I can finish my sentence, Lore rises on her tiptoes and kisses me lightly, catching me completely off guard. My initial surprise causes me to step back and out of her embrace, my mind racing to process the sudden shift in our dynamic.

Lore's gaze drops to the floor, her expression a mix of embarrassment and uncertainty, as the elevator doors open on another floor. A man steps inside with us, oblivious to the charged atmosphere.

Without hesitation, I move to the side, holding the door open for the newcomer, my gaze locked on him. "Get. Out," I order, my tone laced with a sense of urgency.

The man hesitates, glancing from me to Lore, concern etched on his face. "Ma'am, are you okay?"

My patience wears thin as I repeat myself, more forcefully this time. "*Get. Out.*"

Lore nods once, affirming my directive, and the man hastily scurries past me, the elevator doors closing behind him. My arm drops, and I turn back to Lore, our eyes locked in a silent conversation.

She opens her mouth as if to speak but then shakes her head. Without hesitation, I close the gap between us, my fingers gently cradling her face as I lean in and kiss her, our lips meeting in a passionate embrace that speaks volumes about the unspoken connection that has rekindled between us.

Lore's hands entangle in my hair, her body melting into mine. This kiss feels like I'm coming home. It's familiar and comforting, yet it feels like the beginning of so much more.

Deepening the kiss, I walk her backward until I feel the cold, hard wall of the elevator. Lore moans softly, and my cock goes hard as a rock. The years of being apart are suddenly forgotten—my body knows what it wants even if my head is telling me to slow down. The doors open again, and someone coughs, spoiling the moment.

Grabbing Lore's hand, I pull her out of the elevator, through the lobby, and out into the sunshine. My bike is parked near the entrance to the hospital, and I make a beeline for it.

"Dirt," says Lore, but I keep walking. "Dirt," she repeats loudly and tugs on my hand, forcing me to stop.

"Lore, just get on my bike."

She pulls out of my grip. "No."

I take a step toward her, and she takes a step back.

Shaking my head, I grasp her face and look into her eyes. "Tell me you don't feel this. Tell me you haven't missed this, and I'll stop. Lore, get on the bike."

"I can't leave."

"Your motel?"

Lore smirks. "Not happening, biker. You and I are older, wiser, and we know how this will end. I live in Willowbrook Falls, and you live in Tourmaline with the Savage Angels. Neither of us is willing to move. We're both headstrong and, Dirt, I like my life."

"What about for now?"

Lore frowns. "What do you mean?"

"Until you leave, I'm yours, and you're mine. No one else."

"And what happens when I leave?"

"I'll kiss you goodbye and wish you well."

Lore covers my hands with hers. "I don't want it to go sour between us like last time."

"It won't. This time, we know what we're getting ourselves into. You've got your life in Willowbrook, and I have mine here. Can't we, for just this brief amount of time, forget the past and *be* together?"

Lore chews on her bottom lip, then nods. My hands fall from her face, and I once again put her hand in mine and pull her toward my bike. I climb on, but Lore looks from me to the hospital.

"Lore?"

She shakes her head, her hair cascading around her face. Lore's eyes are troubled, and her words carry a weight I can't ignore. "I can't. I can't leave him, not today."

As her words sink in, realization washes through me like a cold wave crashing against the shore. Of course, she can't. If Tobias wakes up and no one is there, how will he feel? The thought is like a punch to the gut, making me instantly empathize with her.

Nodding in understanding, I dismount from the bike and step closer to her, our foreheads almost touching. "You're right. Do you mind if I keep you company?"

She sighs, the tension in her shoulders releasing slightly. "Not at all," she replies, her voice soft. "It'll be nice to have someone to talk to."

Hand in hand, we make our way back to Tobias. When we pull back the curtain to his bed, a man is leaning over him.

He scowls at us, disapproval etched on his face as his eyes drop to where we are still holding hands.

"I should have known," he sneers, his words dripping with bitterness. "You abandoned our son for your own pleasure. Typical."

Anger and frustration course through my veins, and for a moment, I entertain the idea of punching the man in the face. But then Lore squeezes my hand, reminding me of the bigger picture. I take a deep breath and regain my composure.

"Hello, Brooks, it's good to see you too." Lore straightens her shoulders and lifts her chin a little higher, refusing to let his disapproval get to her. "And I'm so glad you *finally* made it."

Brook scoffs. "Not all of us live a transient lifestyle we can abandon at a moment's notice."

My anger flares. "Now, hold on there a minute, buddy."

"Dad?" croaks Tobias.

Lore immediately releases my hand and rushes to her son's side. "Tobias?"

"Mom," he whispers. "Where am I?" his voice trembles with uncertainty.

Lore glances at me. "Get the nurse or a doctor or someone."

Nodding, I stride from his bedside to the nurses' station.

"He's awake!" I state loudly to an older nurse who is doing paperwork.

She looks up at me and smiles. "It's about time. I'll call for the doctor and be right in."

Moving quickly, I stand at the foot of Tobias' bed as his parents hover over him, a mix of relief and concern on their faces.

He looks down at me and smiles. "Hey, Dirt. I must be in a bad way if you're here."

Grinning at him, I shake my head playfully. "It's just a scratch. The ladies love scars."

"Well, you'd know," Tobias teases.

Subconsciously, I run my fingers over the scar that runs from my temple into my hairline, a permanent reminder of a past fight, and then chuckle. "Fuck you."

Brooks clears his throat and moves closer to Tobias, positioning himself between us blocking me from his view. "How do you feel, T?"

Tobias' reply is more serious, a note of concern in his voice. "My left eye isn't working."

"The doctor will be here in a minute," I say.

Brooks stands upright. "Do you need to be here? You aren't family."

Tobias reaches for his father's hand. "Dad, it's cool."

Brooks scowls at me but smiles down at his son. "Whatever you want."

The doctor and a nurse bustle into the room, breaking the tension.

"Everybody out," the doctor declares.

Lore kisses Tobias on the forehead. "We'll be right back."

Brooks chimes in, "Yes, *we* will."

All three of us exit the room, making our way to the waiting room, where Zeke is still keeping watch at his post.

Zeke stands as we approach. "How is he?"

"Awake," I reply with relief in my tone.

Zeke's face breaks into a smile as he puts his hands in his pockets and casually rocks back on his heels. "The man likes to make us sweat, doesn't he?"

Chuckling, I nod. "Yep."

"And who are you two?" asks Brooks.

I extend my hand toward him, introducing us. "I'm Dirt, and this is Zeke. We're friends of your son."

Brooks, with a noticeable disdain in his tone, comments, "Bikers?"

"I prefer to think of us as friends," states Zeke, taking a more diplomatic approach.

Brooks looks down at my hand and reluctantly shakes it. "Brooks Dupont."

"Nice to meet you, but I wish it were under better circumstances."

"That makes two of us."

Lore moves to stand next to me. "I'm glad you're here, Brooks. You and Tobias have a lot to talk about."

Brooks' expression darkens, and he shakes his head with more than a hint of disappointment. "He has too much of you in him. Tobias could have been anything, but instead, he runs a strip club for the underbelly of society."

The tension in the room seems to escalate as the

weight of their unspoken disagreements hangs in the air.

Lore's voice takes on a note of finality as she addresses Brooks. "Not now, not today. You keep your narrow-minded bullshit to yourself. Our son is happy, and that's all I care about."

Brooks inhales a deep breath and then exhales slowly, his frustration palpable. "Do you think he'll still feel this way with one eye? If he hadn't been gallivanting around with bikers, this would *never* have happened."

Zeke barks out a laugh, causing us to turn and stare at him.

"Gallivanting?" Zeke chuckles, shaking his head. "I can't picture Tobias gallivanting. The man is way too big to prance around like a pansy."

The comical image of Tobias in a skirt briefly crosses my mind, and I can't help but laugh. Lore cocks her head to the side in confusion, but as the laughter spreads, she joins in. Brooks, however, seems less amused and moves away from us, clearly irritated.

Still chuckling, I wrap my arms around Lore, sharing the joy of the moment. It's not about finding Tobias' situation funny, it's about the relief of having him awake and on the path to recovery.

CHAPTER
7

LORE

Being held in Dirt's comforting embrace while we share laughter, I feel a sense of belonging. In contrast, Brooks never made me feel this way. Our relationship had always been fraught with difficulties. With him, I never felt like I belonged. I wore the wrong clothes and said the wrong things. He was an amazing father to Tobias, but over the years, whatever he felt for me turned toxic. From the moment I met Dirt, we fell into an easy relationship until we didn't. I wanted more for him and wanted him to leave the Savage Angels. That was when the cracks started to appear in our once-strong bond. Dirt understood me like no man ever has, but he was content in this small town with his MC.

Thinking back, I didn't trust him enough to tell him who Tobias was, and Tobias, for whatever reason, kept my secret. He knew how much I loved Dirt and how hard it was for me to leave.

Brooks clears his throat. I lock eyes with Dirt for a moment before stepping out of his comforting hold. Dirt's expression darkens, but he remains silent.

"I need to talk to Brooks. Will you be okay to wait here?"

Dirt scowls and glances at Brooks, but he nods. "We'll be here when you get back."

Reaching out, I squeeze his hand and whisper, "Thank you." Turning to Brooks, I suggest, "There's a cafeteria downstairs. Let's go get some coffee."

Brooks hesitates before he replies, "I don't want to leave Tobias."

I put on a reassuring smile and coax him gently, "Come on, Brooks. It'll only take a minute. Let's give the doctor some space to do her job. The coffee is awful, but it's on me."

Brooks looks past me to Dirt and Zeke, then turns and walks to the elevator. Smiling at Dirt, I roll my eyes and then follow Brooks.

Inside the elevator, Brooks breaks the silence, "Found another biker?"

Sighing, I say, "You make it sound like I dated a whole MC. There was only ever one biker, and it was Dirt."

"*Great* name," he replies sarcastically.

I roll my eyes. "It's a club name."

Brooks scoffs, his disapproval written all over his face. "Well, I didn't think his mother gave him that name."

The doors open, and he steps out ahead of me, walking in the wrong direction.

"It's this way."

Brooks makes a sharp turn and once again strides ahead, not offering any acknowledgment of my guidance. When I catch up with him, he's standing in line, waiting to be served, so I stand next to him.

"Do you still like your coffee black, no sugar?" Brooks asks, surprising me with his recollection after all these years.

Nodding, I say, "Yes."

He casts a glance at me, raising an eyebrow. "What?"

"It's been years, Brooks. I'm a little surprised you remember."

Brooks' gaze softens as he looks at me. "Some things are hard to forget, Lore."

His words hang in the air, a reminder of the complicated past we share and the emotions that still linger beneath the surface.

Brooks' gaze drops to the floor as we inch forward in the coffee line. "Do you know how it happened?"

"He was at a party. The gunmen were aiming for someone else, and he got in the way."

Brooks rubs his forehead. "I'll never understand why he chooses to work with these people."

As I study Brooks, I notice the signs of aging on his face—the crease marks around his eyes, evidence of a man who has laughed a lot in his life, and his once-blond hair has turned mostly gray, but it suits him, adding a touch of wisdom to his appearance. On his left hand, I spot a silver band, and curiosity gets the best of me.

Reaching out, I tap the metal. "When did you get married?"

"Tobias didn't tell you?"

"No." I shake my head.

The unspoken questions hang in the air, and the weight of our history together feels palpable in the small cafeteria.

He twists the band around his finger, his expression pensive. "I asked him not to tell you, but I'm still surprised he didn't." Brooks puts his hands in his pockets. "Her name is Elizabeth, and we got married a little over a year ago."

"Why didn't you want me to know?"

Brooks shrugs, a touch of bitterness in his tone. "I've been mad at you a long time, Lore. I didn't want you or your lifestyle to infect my relationship with Elizabeth. She knows very little about you."

His words cut deep, and the years of resentment

between us become all too apparent. The strains in our relationship have clearly left lasting scars.

Not wanting to argue with him, I abruptly change the subject. "You were a good father to Tobias." Brooks looks into my eyes. "I'm glad you're happy."

"Happy?" he repeats with a puzzled expression.

"Well, yes. You and I were never a good fit, but you loved and looked after Tobias. He adores you."

"It's your fault we weren't a good fit, Lore, not mine." His words hit me like a punch in the gut.

The harshness of his words surprises me.

"Brooks, we were not a good fit, and it wasn't all on me."

"Actually, *it was*," he counters, unyielding.

The tension between us flares once more, a reminder of the unresolved issues that have simmered beneath the surface for years.

"Now isn't the time to argue. Can't you, for once, just be civil?" I plead with Brooks as we reach the front of the line.

He ignores me as he orders two coffees. I move to the end of the counter, where you pick up your coffee. Brooks pays for our drinks and then stands next to me.

"You were supposed to pay for the coffee."

"You were being a dick, so you got to pay."

Brooks stares straight ahead, his lips going into a hard, thin line. It's a familiar sight. He used to act this way when we were together, and the memory of it stirs up old emotions. Dirt might have his problems, but he never shied away from an argument. With him, I always knew where I stood, but Brooks would give me days of silent treatment, and I hated it. Still do.

"Is Elizabeth with you?" I ask to change the subject.

"Yes," he replies curtly.

"Why didn't you bring her to the hospital?"

"She's waiting at the motel."

"Which one?"

As our coffees are placed in front of us, we both reach for our Styrofoam cups.

He closes his eyes momentarily, then shakes his head. "I can't remember. It's blue."

I take a sip of my coffee. "I'm staying there too."

Brooks spits out his coffee as he coughs. "You can't be serious?" he splutters.

"Pearl isn't exactly a big town, and it is the closest to the hospital. It makes sense you'd choose to stay there too."

He sighs, seemingly flustered. "I'll move."

"Don't be ridiculous." I keep walking back toward the elevators. "It's not like we are in the same room. Besides, I should meet Elizabeth."

Brooks' response is swift and firm. "No. There's no reason for you to meet her."

Confused by his resistance, I ask, "But why?

Brooks, we share a son. For Tobias' sake, I can be nice."

He purses his lips, then walks ahead of me back to the elevator. Standing next to him, I notice a vein throbbing in his temple, a sign of his emotions. The tension between us seems to have no end in sight.

"I'll move. You and Elizabeth can stay in the motel. It's not a big deal."

Brooks' head drops to his chest, and he mutters, "You've been there longer than us. We'll move."

Reaching out, I touch his arm. "Brooks, I don't understand why we can't stay in the same motel."

The elevator doors open, and we step inside. He takes a sip of his coffee, then another while I wait for him to answer.

"It's just easier if you two don't meet," he admits with a frown.

Unwilling to give up, I express my willingness to mend fences. "I know we haven't always gotten along, but Brooks, I'm willing to try."

He shakes his head, his tone final. "Let's focus on Tobias and leave all the personal stuff alone."

As the elevator carries us back to the hospital room, the unresolved tension between us lingers oppressively. Brooks gestures for me to walk in front of him as we exit the elevator.

"I need to speak with Dirt and Zeke."

He huffs out a laugh, shakes his head, and quickly walks away from me. With a sigh, I walk into the waiting room. Zeke is nowhere to be seen, but Dirt is leaning back in a chair, legs stretched out, crossed at the ankles.

"From the look on your face, I can tell the family reunion didn't go well," Dirt observes.

Sitting next to him, I absently take his hand in mine. "If we hadn't had Tobias, we wouldn't even know each other now. Brooks seems determined to make this as difficult as possible."

"There's a fine line between love and hate," Dirt offers.

With a small shake of my head, I turn to look at him. "I never loved Brooks. He is, I mean was... hell, I don't know anymore. I thought he was a good man, but now, at the very sight of me, he does a complete one-eighty. He never even told me he'd gotten married."

Dirt raises an eyebrow and suggests, "Maybe *he* still holds a torch for you?"

Frowning, I dismiss the idea with a wave of my hand. "Lord, no. After Tobias was born, he made it his mission in front of Tobias to always be sweet to me, but if he wasn't in the room, Brooks was awful. The only good thing he ever did was not try to turn Tobias against me. I've never heard him say a bad word about me in front of our son, and I try to do the same."

"Tobias is a grown-assed man. You can't tell me he doesn't know how his parents feel about each other. Did he know his dad had remarried?"

"Brooks told him not to tell me."

"So Tobias knows. The man is very good at reading people. It makes him invaluable at his job."

"Our shared concern for Tobias has always outweighed the bitterness of our past, and we've both strived to keep any disagreements or animosity away from him. It's the one thing we've maintained as a semblance of unity in our separate lives."

Dirt rubs a thumb over the top of my hand. "Tobias will know how Brooks treats you. He's a master when it comes to seeing people for who they really are."

"I should get back."

He raises my hand to his lips, gently placing a kiss. "I'll be here when you're done."

"It could be hours."

Dirt's smile is warm and reassuring. "There's nowhere I'd rather be."

With his unwavering support, I rise from my seat, feeling a sense of determination to face whatever challenges lie ahead with Brooks and Tobias.

CHAPTER
8

DANE

Low voices and classic rock filter through the closed door of the office in the garage, creating a soothing backdrop to my task at hand. I take a sip of bitter coffee and wonder how the hell Addy, who normally does the paperwork, drinks this shit.

Spread out before me is a stack of documents, receipts, and maps. It's time to get organized, and I lean in closer, my rugged hands picking up a pen. The hum of the overhead fan competes with the chatter from the garage floor just outside, but I'm determined to focus on the task at hand. Well, I'm trying to focus.

If I'm being truthful with myself, I'm avoiding going home. The house is currently filled with musicians and their partners, Dave, Kat's manager, and his long-time boyfriend, Luther.

A gentle knock sounds on the closed office door, pulling me back to the present. "Come in."

Kat enters with a wide, infectious smile on her pretty face. She adores having a house full of people, especially when it involves her bandmates.

"Darlin', what are you doing here? Where are the twins?"

Her eyes are bright with excitement, reflecting the joy of the gathering at home. "Grandpa Dave and Luther are looking after them. I came into town to collect pies from Howie and to spend quality alone time with my husband." She winks at me. "If he's not too busy?"

"Are we talking naked quality time?" I tease.

Kat laughs. "Not enough time for that." She moves around the desk, and I push away from it so she can sit in my lap. "Are you okay?"

Wrapping my arms around her, I say, "I'm good."

"Then why are you here doing paperwork when I know you hate it?" She studies my face with a concerned expression.

"It has to be done."

"Addy will do it," Kat presses.

"Sal should arrive today." Kat nods. "And I'd rather he came here to talk than at the house. There's more privacy. I love your band, but they are nosy fuckers."

Kat giggles. "Well, I get it, but they *are* family, and

Sal was the one who drove me into town. He's over in the clubhouse."

"Did he bring Emily with him?"

"Nope, just him and me."

"I'll get Judge to drive you home."

Kat frowns. "I'm perfectly capable."

"Yes, you are. But I'd feel better if you had Judge with you, just in case there are any stalkers in town."

Kat scowls at me but then nods. "Okay. He'll want to come out to the house anyway. Jasmin has arrived."

Scooping her up, I stand and put her butt on the desk, cup her face and kiss her. Our lips meet in a gentle, tender kiss. Kat moans, so I deepen it, our mouths moving together with a fiery connection.

My hands move to her waist, pulling her close. Kat breaks the kiss, and I pepper her face and neck with playful kisses, making her giggle.

"Stop!"

Grinning down at her, I waggle my eyebrows. "You seemed to enjoy yourself. I could keep going?"

With both her hands on my chest, she pushes me away. "You know I love you, but I've got pies to buy and a house full of guests."

"Woman, you're killing me."

Kat slides off the desk and rests her hands on my hips, a mischievous glint in her eyes. "Honey, a quickie in the office isn't going to happen," she says, her smile teasing. "At least not today."

I chuckle, draping an arm around her shoulders, and we walk out of the office and make our way over to the clubhouse. "We have our room in the clubhouse?"

Kat laughs softly, her voice a melodic sound as we cross the parking lot. "House full of guests, remember?"

We enter the clubhouse, and I notice Judge engaged in a conversation with Sal near the bar. The club's atmosphere is alive with the familiar buzz of activity, friends, and a sense of brotherhood that has always been a part of our lives. But with all the new people here, I forget my wife is famous and more than one of the brothers' eyes light up when she enters the room.

Judge sees us approaching and smiles at Kat. "Tell me we are out of here?"

"Yes, you are," I answer for her. "Jas is at the house."

Judge holds up his cell phone. "I know. She texted me an hour ago." He looks at Sal. "Good seeing you, brother. Is Emily with you?"

"Yes, she is out at the house with the children."

King walks over to our little group and holds out a hand to Sal. "I'm King, President of the Savage Angels MC in Las Vegas."

Sal glances at me, then shakes the man's hand. "Salvatore Agostino."

King's grip tightens on Sal's hand, and the tension in the air is palpable. It's clear that Sal's reputation precedes him, and there's an unspoken understanding among the men in the room.

"Sal, let's have a sit-down," I state, and King nods. "Alone."

King scowls at me. "Don't you think I should be in on this conversation?"

I offer a reassuring smile. "You will be, brother, but Sal is family, and I want an update on my sister before we dive into business. I wouldn't want to bore you with the details."

King's scowl softens, and he nods before walking back to the corner he came from.

Judge leans in, his voice hushed, and says, "He's been asking questions about you. Guess he figures since you and I argue that I'm not on team Dane. I set him straight, but I won't be the only one he's talked to. Best keep an eye on him, Prez, and send him home soon."

"Team Dane?"

Judge barks out a laugh. "Yeah, like team vampire or team werewolf?"

"Have you been watching *Twilight* again?" asks Kat with a giggle.

Judge pulls his top lip up to look like a vampire and says, "Team Edward all the way."

Kat laughs harder and goes up on tiptoes to kiss my cheek. "Love you, don't be late." Then she looks at Judge. "Meet you in the car."

We watch her leave the clubhouse before I turn to Judge and say, "Stay close to her. There's too many new faces in town."

Judge rolls his eyes. "You know I don't actually watch *Twilight*, right? And, of course, I'll look after Kat."

With a smirk, I respond, "Sure you don't, *Team Edward.*"

"It's something Jas used to say."

Sal replies, "Of course you don't, my friend. We believe you."

Judge scowls at both of us. "Screw you both."

Sal and I laugh as he jogs after Kat.

"Where can we talk?" asks Sal.

"Yeah, let's go into the chapel. We'll have privacy, but not for long. King will want to be in on this conversation."

"Do you trust him?"

I pause for a moment, considering the question. "I'm not sure."

Sal raises an eyebrow at my uncertainty. "Coming from you, that's a no."

Walking into the chapel, Sal closes the door behind us as I systematically shut all the blinds, ensuring our conversation remains private. We take our seats at the table, with me settling in at the head and Sal to my left.

"What do you know?" I ask, my tone serious and

focused, ready to discuss the matter at hand.

Sal leans back in the chair, his demeanor reflecting the weight of the information he's about to share. "The man I left in charge of our operations in Las Vegas has been helping the Abruzzis. Apparently, they felt their cut wasn't large enough. The old man is trying to squeeze me out."

Sal is a captain in the Abruzzi Crime Family. They are stupid to undercut a loyal member of their family. Sal values loyalty and discretion above all else in matters of business. This betrayal will not sit well with him.

"And the missing MC members?"

Sal clasps his hands on the worn wooden table and looks down at them, his expression dark and concerned. "My man in Vegas... he confessed they have been eliminated. It's a mess, and there's only one course of action for me," he pauses and looks me in the eyes. "For us. We must strike back."

The gravity of the situation settles in, and I can't help but feel a sense of urgency. This is more than just a power struggle—it's a threat to our brotherhood.

"Do they know you know?"

Sal spreads his hand out and drags his shoulder up in a shrug. "Maybe? Probably? My man in Vegas has been removed, so they'll be wondering what happened to him."

Without saying it out loud, I understand Sal has

dealt with the problem decisively. We've worked together for years now, and I know his men are loyal to him. For one of them to betray Sal would have cut deep, and for Sal to take such a drastic step would have shaken his trust in those closest to him, perhaps even me.

"Do you have doubts, brother?" I search his eyes for any signs of uncertainty.

Sal inhales and exhales slowly, his nostrils flaring. "About you? No. About some members of your MC? Perhaps."

The tension in the room deepens as we contemplate the challenges ahead. It's clear that the Abruzzis have not only infiltrated our territory but have sowed seeds of doubt and discord among our own ranks. This is a battle we can't afford to lose for the sake of our brotherhood and the safety of our loved ones.

"What are we going to do going forward?"

Salvatore smiles at me, and if I didn't know him, I'd swear he was getting ready to kill me.

"We wait," he says, his voice carrying a sinister undercurrent. "Right now, they are filling their ranks to overthrow us, but there are still those in the Abruzzi ranks who will not cross me *or you*. We need to find those who are loyal, and when the time is right, we'll strike."

"War?" The word comes out of my mouth and leaves a bitterness in its wake.

It's been many years since we've had bloodshed with our rivals. I had hoped I could keep the dogs of war at bay for the rest of my presidency. I'm older with a young family, and I have a lot to lose. The prospect of conflict hangs heavy in the air, and I can't help but worry about the price that will be paid.

CHAPTER
9

DIRT

Taking the stairs two at a time, I enter the clubhouse, immediately sensing the charged atmosphere within. The chapel's door is closed, and the blinds are drawn, creating an aura of secrecy and tension. In one corner, King sits with some of his men and a few of our members, all fixated on the chapel's wooden door.

Jonas walks in behind me, and he also feels the tension. He cocks his head to the side and raises his eyebrows.

"Buy you a drink?"

"Yeah."

We both nod at King, who gives us a chin lift. Standing side by side at the bar, Rebel puts two glasses in front of us and fills them with whiskey.

I twirl the glass in my hand, staring at the amber liquid. "Reb, things seem a bit tense?"

Rebel doesn't meet my gaze but keeps his head down and wipes the glassware. "Dane and Sal are in the chapel. King was not invited to the talks. Seems like he's not happy."

Rebel walks away from us, and Jonas and I exchange a knowing look, then turn our attention to King, who appears to be simmering with frustration on the other side of the room. The tension within the clubhouse is palpable.

The chapel door opens, and Dane and Sal emerge, both wearing smiles. Dane looks at me, and I raise my glass in a silent greeting. King rises from his chair, his face flushed with what I perceive as anger. Wanting to diffuse the situation, I walk to the center of the room and raise my glass in the air.

"Brothers!" I bellow, stomping my feet for emphasis. The room falls silent, all eyes on me. "I have good news. Tobias is awake."

"Damn," Jonas says, sidling up next to me. "You sure know how to work a room."

"Thanks," I reply, watching as King reluctantly eases back into his chair. But even as he raises his glass in toast, I can't shake the feeling that this is far from over.

"Damn straight!" someone shouts, raising their glass in a toast to Tobias' recovery.

The atmosphere in the room instantly shifts at

my declaration. The tension is replaced with cheers, and King raises his glass higher, then takes a sip. His eyes drift from me to Dane, and his lips turn down. The man clearly wants to take what Dane has earned, but for as long as I'm this chapter's Sergeant at Arms, that's never going to happen.

"Hey," Dane says, appearing at my side. The warmth of his hand on my back is a welcome contrast to the cold air that seems to radiate from King. "That's great news about Tobias."

"Sure is," I reply, unable to keep the triumphant grin from spreading across my face. "He's one tough son of a bitch."

"Always has been," Dane agrees, clapping me on the shoulder once more before stepping away. "Let's celebrate? This calls for a round of drinks on me."

"Sounds like a plan." I nod, already feeling lighter, as though the weight of the past few days has been lifted from my shoulders.

But as I watch King in the corner of my eye, a shadow of unease still lingers. I know this reprieve is only temporary—the storm may have been diverted, but it still brews on the horizon.

"Cheers to Tobias' recovery and to the battles that lie ahead," Jonas says, sliding up next to me and clinking his glass against mine with a grin. "To Tobias."

"Cheers," I echo, and we drink to our brother.

It's late when I enter the hospital, the harsh fluorescent lights overhead casting an eerie glow on the sterile, white-washed walls.

"Evening," the security guard grunts with a slight lift of his chin, barely looking up from his desk as I pass.

I nod back, thankful for the lack of conversation tonight. The elevator doors open with an eerie silence. Stepping out onto the floor Tobias is on, I make my way to the dimly lit waiting room. Kade is there, hunched over, engrossed in his cell phone, the soft blue glow of the screen illuminating his tired face.

"Reading or playing a game?" I ask, my voice a hushed murmur in the otherwise quiet room.

Kade startles slightly, shoving his phone into his pocket. "A game."

"Any change?"

"The doctors are happy. He's awake, talking, and even had a meal. Tell me you're here to relieve me?" Kade scrubs a hand down his face.

"Sorry, brother," I reply with a half smile. "I've

come to see Tobias and maybe convince his mother to leave the hospital for a few hours."

Kade smirks knowingly. "She's a good-looking woman."

I shoot him a warning look. "Watch yourself, blondie."

Kade chuckles, and I head for Tobias' room, the soft sound of my footsteps echoing on the hard linoleum floors. When I enter the room, both Lore and Tobias are staring at me, their eyes heavy with fatigue and worry.

"Hey, man, how are you feeling?" I approach Tobias' bed, offering a reassuring smile as I rest a hand on his mother's shoulder.

Tobias manages a weak grin. "Like I got shot."

I can't help but chuckle. "Been there, done that," I respond, my gaze shifting to Lore. "How are you holding up?"

Lore lets out a deep sigh, relief evident in her tired eyes. "Relieved."

Tobias reaches out and pats his mother's hand. "You should go get some sleep. Dad will be back any minute."

A frown creases Lore's forehead. "We aren't that bad, are we?"

"Mom, you don't fight..." Tobias begins, "... but I can tell it's difficult for you both to be in the same room. Go, get some sleep." His eyes shift to me. "Take her to the motel, will you?"

Lore hesitates, her gaze flickering between her son and me. It's clear she wants nothing more than to stay by Tobias' side, but exhaustion is etched into the lines of her face, betraying her need for sleep.

"Mom, it's okay," Tobias interjects, his voice warm and reassuring. "I'll be fine. You need to take care of yourself too."

"Come on," I say softly, holding out a hand toward Lore. "Just a couple of hours. We'll be back before you know it."

After a moment that seemed to stretch into eternity, she finally nods, her fingers slipping into mine with a sigh of resignation. As we walk away, I glance back at Tobias, his face pale and drawn, surrounded by the sterile walls of the hospital room. His hand touches the patch over his eye, and I wonder how he feels about losing it and his hair.

"Thank you," Lore whispers, her voice barely audible above the din of my thoughts. "For coming back. For everything."

"Always," I replied, my voice soft but resolute.

We make our way to the waiting room, where Kade stands by the window, his tall frame silhouetted against the dim glow of lights outside, his hair is tousled and covering half of his face. He must have sensed our approach as he turns his gaze toward us, sweeping his hair out of his eyes.

"Want me to go sit with him?"

"No, I think he needs a little space."

Lore shakes her head, her brow furrowing. "Not too much space. He needs to come to terms with losing his eye, but he also needs to realize how lucky he is. I don't want him spending too much time in his own head. Give him an hour, then go on in."

"Will do." Kade pulls his cell phone out of his pocket and holds it up. "Put your number in my phone in case anything happens."

Lore nods and takes it off him. With a few taps, she hands it back.

Kade looks down at his phone and smiles. "Tobias' Badass Mother? I like it."

Lore smiles, the first real one I've seen since I arrived. "Figured you could use a little humor right now."

Kade grins. "Night shifts are the worst."

Lore looks at me. "You know he could go home."

"No," replies Kade. "One of us will always be here. We owe Tobias that much."

Lore stifles a yawn. "Thank you."

"Take her home, Dirt. She's beat."

Tugging on her hand, I pull her from the waiting room to the elevator and out of the hospital.

"Did you drive?"

Lore shakes her head. "No, I walked today. I was hoping you'd come and get me."

Her words warm my heart. "Come and meet my baby."

With my arm around Lore, I guide her to my Harley.

"Here she is," I announce, even though there's not another motorcycle parked anywhere near us.

"Wow, she sure is beautiful." Lore circles the motorcycle, her fingers hovering over the glossy white details, never quite touching them. "Is this a fifty-eight?"

"Sure is." I move closer to the bike and climb on. "Need a lift?"

Lore laughs, puts her hand in mine, and swings her leg over the bike, settling in behind me. Her hands find their way to my waist, fingers gripping the fabric of my jacket as she presses herself close.

"It's been a long time since I've ridden on the back of a bike."

Twisting in the seat, I look over my shoulder at her. "Really?"

Lore nods. "Yep. The last time I rode was with you."

With a kickstart and the flick of my wrist, she roars to life, a powerful purr that vibrates through our bodies. Lore's warmth pressed against my back feels so right, something I haven't felt in a long time. As we race through the empty streets, the wind whipping past us, I revel in the sensation of freedom.

In this moment, with Lore's arms wrapped

around me and the wind in my hair, I feel alive. Complete. And I'll do whatever it takes to hold on to this feeling, to protect the fragile bond that has blossomed between us. Because deep down, I know that Lore is my missing piece—the one thing I've been searching for all these years.

The neon lights of the motel flicker as we pull into the parking lot, casting an eerie glow on the cracked asphalt. Lore points to where her rental is, and I park behind it.

"Thanks for the ride," she says, hopping off the bike before I've barely come to a complete stop. Her legs are steady, and she stands tall, the wind dancing through her hair.

I can't help but wish she wasn't so eager to leave my side.

"Anytime," I say, trying to sound casual.

The truth is, I want more time with her to get to know her better and understand the secrets buried deep within her eyes.

"Can I interest you in a drink?"

Not needing to be asked twice, I kill the engine, and silence settles over the small parking lot.

Lore digs through her purse and finds the key to her room. She fumbles with it in the lock but gets the door open. Once inside, she flips on a light. The walls are painted an optimistic shade of yellow, trying to breathe life into the old bones of this motel. A large, queen-size bed sits against the far wall, the bright red comforter neatly tucked around the edges, accentuated by a couple of crisp, white pillows. The carpet beneath my feet is slightly threadbare but clean like it's been vacuumed meticulously every day for decades.

As I step farther inside, I notice more details that add to the place's charm—a rickety wooden desk adorned with a kitschy lamp and a rotary phone, a dresser topped with a small television that must be older than me. The curtains are drawn, giving us a sense of privacy.

I close the door behind me and stare at Lore. "Man, they don't make 'em like this anymore."

Lore laughs. "There's a reason for that." She looks around the room. "But it's very clean and not hugely expensive."

Opening the mini refrigerator, she looks at me and says, "I'm afraid all I can offer you is water or Coke." A yawn escapes her, and she shakes her head.

"You're tired. I should go."

Lore sits on the edge of the bed, the springs squeaking beneath her. "Stay."

"You're beat."

She tilts her head to the side and smiles. "I am, but I don't want you to go. Stay with me. I'll sleep better if you're here."

"I can do that."

Kicking off my boots, I unbuckle my jeans and let

them fall to the floor, then take off my cut and T-shirt.

Lore stands. "I'm going to brush my teeth. Be right back."

I reach out and flick the light switch, surrendering the room to shadows, but the bathroom light spills into the space, revealing just enough to prevent me from tripping over my own feet. Moving closer to the bed, I pull back the red comforter and top sheet and climb in, my weight causing the mattress to squeak beneath me.

"I'm done," Lore announces, and I look up to see her standing in the doorway.

She's dressed only in an old, worn T-shirt, the fabric hanging loosely around her body, reaching midthigh. Her legs are bare, and I can't help but let my eyes wander over the smooth expanse of skin, drinking in the sight of her. She pulls the bathroom door but doesn't close it, so the room still has some light, then saunters over to the bed. I scoot over and hold up the comforter and sheet.

"You look beautiful," I tell her honestly, my voice low and husky as I reach out to touch her arm.

She smiles, unable to conceal the pink flush that spreads across her cheeks. "Thank you," she murmurs, slipping beneath the covers and curling up beside me.

I wrap an arm around her, pulling her close, intoxicated by the scent of her skin. My body aches to be closer, to make love to her, but as her breathing slows and deepens, I can tell she's exhausted from the long days spent beside Tobias' bed.

Brushing my lips against her neck, I say, "Goodnight, Lore."

"Night, Dirt."

Within moments, she's asleep.

And as I lay there, listening to her, I wish I could find a way for her and me to stay like this forever.

The pounding on the door echoes through my dreams, pulling me back into reality. My eyes flutter open, and I'm greeted by the sight of Lore's face mere inches from mine. Her eyelashes rest gently against her cheeks, and her lips are slightly parted as she breathes softly in sleep. The warmth of her body is pressed up against mine, her arm draped over my waist.

"Lore!" a voice coming from outside breaks the peace, then he pounds on the door again.

"Brooks?" Lore mumbles, rubbing her eyes and sitting up in bed. She looks as disheveled as I feel, her long brown hair with blonde highlights is a tangled mess. Lore stumbles out of bed and throws open the door. "Is Tobias okay?"

"What?" Brooks asks.

"You're pounding on my door at God knows what time... is my son all right?"

Brooks looks at me and says, "*Our* son is fine."

Crawling out from under the covers, I stand and walk over to my jeans that are still on the floor.

"Why are you here, Brooks?"

"Never mind, I can see you're... busy."

Lore glances over her shoulder, then walks outside and shuts the door. Their voices turn into this muffled buzz outside, and I'm left clueless about the drama unfolding. I pull on my jeans and walk into the bathroom to relieve myself and splash water on my face.

I put on my T-shirt, cut, and finally, my boots. Their conversation is still buzzing outside. I catch a few words, but it's like trying to decode a radio station on the fritz. Not being known for being subtle, I open the door. Lore has her hands on her hips, her face red with anger.

"Is everything okay?" I ask Lore.

She glares at Brooks and says, "Everything is fine."

Brooks shakes his head in frustration and storms away.

Lore pushes past me, settling on the edge of the bed with a heavy sigh. "He's an ass."

Closing the door behind me, I join her on the bed. "Yeah, he is. What did he want?"

Lore runs a hand through her hair and gives me a half smile. "He doesn't approve of my life choices."

I raise an eyebrow. "So, is that your subtle way of saying Brooks doesn't like me? Because he's made that pretty clear since the day we met."

Lore laughs, placing a comforting hand on my knee. "I'm sorry. This is not how I envisioned us waking up."

Waggling my eyebrows playfully, I ask, "And how did you envision us waking up?"

Lore bumps her shoulder against mine, a sly smile on her lips. "I think you know."

I shoot back with a grin, "The day is young..."

Lore stands and heads toward the bathroom. "Unfortunately, I need to get back to Tobias."

"I could buy you breakfast?" I suggest.

She leans against the door frame. "Yes, so long as it's not in the hospital cafeteria."

Chuckling, I nod. "There's a nice diner not far. It's been a while, but they used to make a good breakfast."

"You don't come to Pearl often?"

"No need. Tourmaline has everything I need."

Lore nods, her face clouding over, then closes the bathroom door.

Walking outside, I find Brooks smoking as he stares at my bike. He takes a drag from his cigarette, the smoke curling around him. His gaze remains fixated on my bike, his fingers tapping rhythmically against the chrome handlebars.

"She's a beauty, hey?"

He flicks the cigarette, sending ashes to the ground, and shrugs. "I wouldn't know." Brooks sighs. "She was never the same after you."

"Excuse me?"

Brooks drops the cigarette and grinds it into the ground. "Lore is a force of nature but a predictable one. Before you, she would come and go out of my life, and I didn't mind. Together we had Tobias, and he bound us, but after you, she never came back for me. Lore only came for our son. I'd always hoped she'd return to me, but you somehow ended us."

"How's your wife?" I ask.

Brooks gives me a sad smile and replies, "Asleep." His gaze goes to a closed door of the motel.

"Maybe you should be with her instead of wishing for something that was never yours."

He scowls at me. "What does some biker have that I don't?"

I shoot back, "For one, I've never talked down to her, and two, I tried to hold on to her but realized Lore needs to find her own path." I give him a once-over. "She seems to be in a good space now. Even with all the shit with Tobias."

Brooks rocks back on his heels, considering my

words. "She does seem more settled. Life in Willowbrook agrees with her."

Lore steps out of the motel room, a smile playing on her lips. However, it quickly fades as she takes in the scene with Brooks and me. "Is everything okay?"

I give her a reassuring grin. "Yeah, babe, Brooks and I were just shootin' the shit. You ready to get something to eat?"

"Starving."

Brooks steps back. "I'll see you later at the hospital. I'll be in after lunch."

Climbing on the bike, I fire her up, the low rumble echoing in the quiet parking lot, and extend a hand to Lore. She gets on, her hands clutching my hips. Brooks watches her for a moment, a mix of emotions flickering across his face before he turns and heads back into his motel room.

The comforting aroma of coffee surrounds us as we sit in the worn vinyl seats in a corner booth of the diner. The morning sunlight filtering through faded curtains and the clinking of cutlery and hum of conversations create a calming backdrop.

Lore's fingers trace patterns on the coffee mug in front of her, her eyes flicking between the menu and the worn tabletop. I study her and the way her hair catches the morning light, framing a face that carries both strength and vulnerability.

The waitress, an older woman with a pen behind her ear, takes our orders. "Okay, so pancakes, bacon, and maple syrup for two, right?"

"Yep," I reply, and Lore nods.

She refills our coffee cups before the waitress walks our order back.

The diner door swings open, and the atmosphere shifts. Turning, I see King stride in with an air of authority. His presence is both commanding and unsettling, the leather cut adorned with patches a testament to the power he holds.

Lore's posture changes slightly as she glances toward him, her eyes narrowing briefly before she looks away. My hand instinctively reaches out, and I rub my thumb over her knuckles.

King saunters over, a predatory confidence in his stride. "Well, well, look who we have here," he drawls, his gaze lingering on Lore. "Dirt, sharing a meal with such a lovely lady. Must be my lucky day."

A ripple of discomfort courses through me, but I keep my expression neutral. "King," I acknowledge, my voice steady.

Lore shifts uncomfortably across from me, her

eyes avoiding his lingering gaze.

He smirks, undeterred by my lack of enthusiasm. "Mind if I join you? Always a pleasure to be in the company of a beautiful woman."

I glance at Lore, my protective instincts kicking in. "We're good, King. Just enjoying a quiet breakfast."

He leans in. "Well, if you change your mind, you know where to find me." With a final look at Lore, he strolls away.

I exhale a breath I didn't realize I was holding, my gaze fixed on King until he disappears farther into the diner.

Lore's eyes meet mine. "Who was that?"

"King, Las Vegas president."

"He's a long way from home. Why would a chapter president come here?"

I take a deep breath as the weight of the truth settles in my chest. "To cause shit. The fucker is after Dane's crown."

"Does he have a cause?"

Moments like these make me realize how much I've missed Lore. She knows the inner workings of an MC, and I don't need to explain anything about club life to her.

"No. But there's trouble coming. Dane has called a meeting out at the barn. Only patched-in Tourmaline members have been invited."

"Does King know?"

Frowning, I say, "He shouldn't know, but I think there's unrest within our ranks."

Lore chews on her bottom lip. "Why the barn?"

"It's our safe place."

Lore chokes on her coffee. "It's the place you *eliminate* problems."

"Yeah, but it's safe from prying eyes."

CHAPTER
10

SALVATORE AGOSTINO
Captain, Abruzzi Crime Family

The door's hinges gave a faint creak as I eased it open, its worn wood protesting the intrusion into the silence that had settled over the house. The narrow sliver of light from the hallway cast a soft glow across the bedroom floor, illuminating the small, scattered toys my children had abandoned earlier in the day. As I stepped out, I took care to avoid the squeaky floorboard by the doorway—my wife is a light sleeper, and the last thing I need is to wake her.

Tony, my second-in-command, is sitting outside our door. He has a book in his hands, which he closes when his dark eyes catch mine. A warm smile spreads across his lips. "I'll watch them as they sleep," he says, nodding toward the closed bedroom door.

There's no one I trust more to keep my family safe.

"Thanks, Tony."

"The others have arrived. They're downstairs."

Stopping, I straighten my long-sleeved shirt, tugging at the cuffs. "All of them?"

"You called them, and they came." Tony stands. "I'm going to do a walk around the outside on this floor, make sure everything is kosher." He lays the book on his seat. "Who would have thought a biker would own a three-story home with multiple points of entry?" Tony taps his temple. "Not very smart of him, boss."

"I guess he didn't think war would come this close to home."

Tony shrugs. "You wouldn't make that mistake."

He walks to the end of the hall, opens the door to the veranda, and steps out.

"Stay sharp," I call out to Tony, my voice barely above a whisper. He nods once before disappearing into the shadows, leaving me to confront the gathering downstairs.

Tony is right. There are too many entrances to this house. It's not a fortress like our home in Chicago. Even if someone managed to get inside, we have a panic room, so I know my family will always be safe.

The fact my closest men have all made the journey here means they all know of Don Abruzzi's betrayal. Walking into the kitchen, sitting around the dining table are Lorenzo, Marco, Stefano, Jonas, and Dane, who sits at the head.

"Thank you all for coming," I begin, my voice low but firm. "I know how much you've sacrificed to be here."

Lorenzo stands and briefly embraces me. "We would burn it all down a hundred times over to be here with you." He lets me go and resumes his seat.

"Can I get you a coffee, Sal?" Dane asks.

"I'll get it."

Opening a cupboard, I pull out a mug, pour myself a cup, and take my seat at the other end of Dane's table.

"What's the plan?" Stefano asks.

"I'm just waiting on a call. Until then, we sit, we talk, and we wait." Dane leans back in his chair.

Most of the men at this table answer to me, so understandably, Marco clears his throat and looks me in the eye.

"Sal?"

Wanting to appear as though we are a united front, I nod. "This is Dane's home, his town, and he's who alerted us to Don Abruzzi's betrayal. So, we do as he says."

Lorenzo raises his eyebrows and states,

"Waiting isn't my strong suit."

Marco barks out a laugh. "If you hadn't told us, I would never have known."

Sitting forward, Lorenzo scowls at him. "Like you're any better at sitting around."

Marco drags a shoulder up to his ear, takes a sip of his coffee, and winces. "This tastes like dirty dish water." He looks at Dane. "Do you have ground coffee beans? I'll make another pot."

"Tastes fine to me," replies Jonas as he slurps the brown liquid.

Marco frowns. "Do you have no taste buds at all?"

Dane's phone rings, and we all lean forward. "Yes?" He looks at me and nods. "Excellent" Dane ends the call. "We're good to go."

Stefano claps his hands together. "Ahh, it's nice when things come together. A road trip?"

Dane rises. "Yeah." He carries his cup to the sink. "Jonas, make sure those who are left behind are *with us*, yeah?"

"I vetted them myself. We can trust them," Jonas replies with conviction.

"Good. Sal, you ready?"

"Our families are safe?"

Dane shifts his weight, his posture tense as he meets my gaze. The moment stretches out between us, heavy with unspoken fears.

Finally, Dane speaks, his words carefully

measured, "I've made sure they're protected. We've got people guarding them around the clock."

Marco barks out a laugh. "And don't forget Tony. He'd use his last breath to protect your wife and children."

Ignoring Marco, I say, "All right." I stand, straightening my spine and squaring my shoulders. "Let's do this."

The others rise to join me, each man grappling with his own demons as they prepare for the conversations ahead.

As we file out of the room, I can't help but glance at an older photograph in the corner—the faces of my wife and children smiling back at me.

The barn looms in the distance, a large building in the middle of the forest. I tighten my grip on the armrest as we approach.

The last time I was here, the echoes of gunfire still reverberate in my mind. It's a place marred by decisions that can't be undone. I killed Guido. The crack of the gun split the air as my bullet found its mark. He was as good as dead already, but it was my hand that snuffed the life out of him.

We stop at the barn's entrance, the air thick with the heavy weight of memories weighing me down. Its weathered walls hold many secrets. The crunch of gravel beneath my shoes echoes in the stillness as I climb out of the car.

The door creaks open, and I'm the first to step inside. Dim light casts long shadows across the familiar, worn-out floor covered in plastic. It makes cleanup a hell of a lot easier as no blood will soak into the wood or the ground beneath us. This place has witnessed the darker side of the Savage Angels. I glance at the spot where Guido fell and feel nothing for him.

The memories intensify as I make my way farther into the barn. This was where I confronted Johnnie, the rage that boiled within me as I protected what was mine. The air in here feels charged with each step as I journey through the choices I made on that fateful night. The ghosts of those moments linger in the air, and I can almost hear the echoes of gunfire. Taking a deep breath, I clear my head and let those memories fade.

"Sal, you okay?" asks Lorenzo.

"Yeah, remembering long-dead ghosts."

He nods. "The plastic on the floor is a bit disturbing."

"It's for easy clean up."

Lorenzo's lips turn down as he stares at the floor. "Makes me uneasy."

Laughing, I slap him on the shoulder. "Don't get shot, and you'll be fine." Walking farther in, a large round table with chairs positioned around it is at the back. "Come, it's time to talk and lay our cards on the table."

Dirt sits at the table, his casual demeanor belies the gravity of our situation. As I approach, he greets me with a nonchalant chin lift, a silent invitation to join him. "Hey, Sal, take a seat. How's the wife and kids?"

"Good."

Dirt smiles. "Crazy times, hey?"

"I wish things were different."

He frowns. "With your family?"

"No. With the Abruzzis. My wife and children are the reason I do what I do to give them the best life. But now? Now, war is coming, and I'm putting them at risk."

Dirt shifts in his seat. "You could walk away."

Surprised he would even suggest such a thing, I shake my head. "No, I can't. Once you're in, you're in. I'm too young to retire, and the family would never allow me to do that. I could no more walk away from this than you could with your MC."

Dirt's eyes widen and, for a moment, he freezes, then nods. "Yeah, I guess so."

His response catches me off guard. Someone entrenched in the lifestyle of a motorcycle club, holding a position of power as the sergeant at arms seems an unlikely candidate for such contemplation.

"Do you ever think about leaving?" I ask as I'm now curious about the man behind the cut, wondering if his loyalty to the club ever waivers.

Dirt opens his mouth to speak, but Dane enters the room, clapping his hands loudly.

"Almost everyone is here. If you haven't already, introduce yourselves. There's not a person in this room I don't trust." Dane's gaze sweeps over my men. "Even the newcomers."

"Who are we waiting on?" Stefano asks.

"Bear, Rebel, and Keg. They shouldn't be too far away."

Jonas sits opposite me, and Dane takes the chair beside him. We are all silent as we sit around the table, each of us lost in our own thoughts. A car door sounds from outside, and Dane looks beyond the table to the barn's entry.

Bear is the first to enter, and since the last time I saw him, he's lost an incredible amount of weight. Next is Rebel, and finally Keg.

"Were you followed?" Jonas asks.

Rebel shakes his head. "No, but we took the long way to make sure. It's why we're late."

They each take a seat, and Dane clears his throat to garner everyone's attention. "What we know so far is that King let certain things slip in Vegas, and as a result, it looks as though the Abruzzi family is muscling in."

Keg, his gaze sharp, adds, "Don't forget about our missing brothers. We're all fairly certain they're dead." His accusatory tone is directed at me.

"I had nothing to do with that," I defend myself, but Keg's steely stare remains fixed on me. Unperturbed, he crosses his arms and leans back in his chair, a silent challenge.

Dane intervenes, lifting a hand to silence me, addressing his man firmly, "Keg, Sal isn't the enemy here. I trust him with my life, just like I trust you."

"Just 'cause he married your sister, don't make him family," Keg retorts, unyielding in his skepticism.

Lorenzo, ever the volatile presence, cracks his neck from side to side—an unmistakable sign that he's gearing up for a confrontation.

"I understand your fears. Do not mistake me for Don Abruzzi. I am a man of my word, and I have to disagree with you. Marrying Dane's sister does indeed make me family. You've seen me around the club, invested my own money into our ventures, and there's nothing I wouldn't do for the club and my men." My response is measured and directed solely at Keg.

Keg's tense posture eases as he uncrosses his arms. "All of this has me on edge. I meant no disrespect. Is there any way we can resolve this without bloodshed?"

"I can't see it going any other way," replies Jonas. "You said it yourself, Keg, we have members missing. Blood must be avenged with blood, and we need to send a clear message. You take *one* of ours, and we take *one hundred* of yours."

Dane holds up his hands. "Okay, let's slow this down. Sal, what do you know?"

"The deal with the Abruzzis and the families in Vegas has always been tenuous. They get a cut as is our way, but they've gotten greedy. For some time, the Don has expressed his dissatisfaction with my marriage to your sister and my business involvements with the Savage Angels."

Marco leans forward and stares me in the eyes. "It's true. Don Abruzzi, in his roundabout way, was asking me if I was willing to take on your territory in Chicago. When I pointed out it was yours, he chuckled, said he was an old man, and was confused, but now that I think on it, he was sounding me out."

"You're not the only one who's had a conversation with the Don," Stefano says.

"Me too," states Lorenzo.

"And yet none of you came to me?" Frustration is evident in my tone.

Lorenzo clasps his hands together on the table. "There was no need, boss. None of us would ever betray you. I'm sure the others thought the Don was testing us to make sure we are loyal. Which we are."

The room holds a tense pause, the unspoken loyalty of my men resonating in the air. Despite the clandestine conversations with the Don, there's an implicit understanding among us that loyalty remains unwavering, and the unity of our brotherhood is not easily shaken.

"How are we going to handle this?" Dane asks.

Rising from my seat, I sweep my gaze across the table, fixing my eyes on Jonas. "I acknowledge losing members is unforgivable, and I understand the impulse for vengeance," I say, pausing for emphasis. "But we all stand to lose a great deal. Beyond our investments, we each have families. The Abruzzis are seeking war, and historically, they've eradicated entire families to stave off future conflict. They've been cautious thus far, not yet ready for an outright war, but they are preparing for one. If you permit me, I can negotiate with the other families and assess who can be trusted and who stands with us. Only then should we consider taking action."

Dane stands. "We have a larger problem within our ranks." He leans forward over the table, resting his hands on it. "I believe King is working with the Abruzzis. It's the only way they could have driven us out. They have to have an inside connection."

Keg shakes his head. "No. He's one of *us*."

Dirt points at Keg. "Brother, I get where you're coming from, but I think Dane is right. I've got feelers out trying to verify what I believe to be true, which is King looking out for King."

"When you get definite proof, I'll back you, but are we really saying we think a chapter president has turned against us?" He shakes his head. "I don't believe it."

Dane's gaze fixates on Keg, and I see concern and uncertainty etched across his face. "Keg, this is all between us. Outside this room, no one knows our intentions, and I certainly wouldn't accuse King in public unless I had proof. But I'm telling you, it doesn't look good."

Rebel interrupts by clearing his throat. "I've spent time with the chapter in Vegas. I'm with Keg on this one. King is an arrogant SOB, and it's clear he wants Tourmaline, but I don't think he'd betray us." Rebel shifts his attention to Dirt. "Could someone else close to him be pulling the strings?"

"Firstly, how do you know he's after Tourmaline?" Dirt leans in, his expression intense.

"He's challenged Dane on more than one occasion, and when Dane and Sal had a meeting without him, he just about blew a gasket."

Dirt leans back, seemingly processing the information. "Secondly, who else could it be? His VP? His sergeant at arms? And just so everyone here is crystal fucking clear on my stance, if by some miracle King becomes Tourmaline's president, I'm fucking out."

I sink heavily into my seat while Dane looks at Dirt with raised eyebrows.

Rebel shrugs. "It has to be someone higher up in the MC. If it's not King, it has to be the VP. King's sergeant at arms is like you, Dirt... loyal to a fault."

Dane stares at the table, and a palpable tension fills the room as all eyes are on him.

Slowly, he eases back into his seat, and his gaze locks with mine. "Maybe I've been approaching this the wrong way? Reb might have a point," he admits, his attention shifting to Dirt. "Dig into everything you can about his VP. And, Dirt, I know you don't need me to spell it out for you, but I will anyway... keep it discreet."

"Are you telling me to back off of King?"

"No," Dane replies, clenching his teeth. "But maybe my judgment is clouded when it comes to him. He takes every opportunity to challenge me in public, like Rebel said, but that doesn't mean he's the one."

"Agreed," I interject.

"I need a drink," declares Jonas.

"Count me in," chimes in Marco.

Rebel stands, opens a door at the back of the barn, and walks through it.

He sticks his head back through the doorway and looks at Marco. "Lend me a hand?" Marco nods and rises. "Does everyone like whiskey?"

"Have we got vodka back there?" Jonas asks.

"Pussy," Dane teases with a smirk.

"It's a damn sight better drink than the piss you drink," Jonas fires back.

Dane laughs, and the tension in the room eases. Even Keg cracks a smile.

Marco reenters the room, placing eight glasses on the table. Following him, Rebel returns with additional glasses and a bottle under each arm.

When everyone has a drink before them, Dane lifts his glass. "To us, may those who betray us get what they deserve."

We all take a sip, cementing the bond between us.

Bear finishes his whiskey in a single gulp and then slams the empty glass on the table. "Prez, I know it's not my place to question you, but…" he pauses, looking at Dane.

"It's a round table for a reason, Bear. We all have a voice here."

"I think you need to talk to King. I'm not saying we accuse him of betraying us, but I think you need to have a sit-down with him and Sal and lay out some of our cards. It'd be good to see his reaction." He raises his chin toward Keg. "As much as I don't like King, Keg has a point."

Dane looks thoughtful, his jaw set as he weighs up Bear's words.

"I'm on the same page as Bear," I remark, lifting my glass for another sip. "If we give the impression that it's not about questioning his loyalty but rather someone close to him, he might either make a reckless move, thinking we trust him, or he'll scrutinize his own men more closely."

"I think it's risky," Dirt interjects, tossing back the remnants of his drink. He sets the empty glass down with a decisive thud, his expression betraying a mix of skepticism and concern.

I nod. "True, it's not without its dangers. But the greater risk might be letting this uncertainty fester in the dark. We need to bring things to light, even if it means dancing on the edge for a while."

Dane taps the table. "Okay, Sal and I will have a sit-down with King." He gestures toward Dirt. "You'll dive into his VP."

"My men will feel out the families we have business dealings with, but the Abruzzis are the most powerful in our organization. Some will side with the Don simply because of that," I add.

Lorenzo says, "The Santoros hate the Abruzzis as do the Bianchis. I'm sure they'll side with us. Marco, you have dealings with the Fontanas... if war comes, will they side with us?"

Marco's lips tighten. "The Fontanas will do what's best for the Fontanas. Always have."

"Same with the Lombardis, but they hate Sal, so just to spite him, they'd side with the Abruzzis."

It's true the Lombardis have a profitable working relationship with the Abruzzis. I've disrespected Don Matteo by excluding him from deals in Chicago, and the Donati family in Las Vegas still harbors a grudge. These three families hold significant influence, and if I attempt to supplant the Abruzzis as the dominant force, it will probably ignite a war to determine who holds power over us all.

Dane's voice cuts through my thoughts. "Sal, is there anything else we need to discuss?"

"There is one way to get the Donatis on our side."

Dane's immediate response is a firm shake of his head. "No."

"If we cut them in on the casinos, they will join us. They value the dollar more highly than even their children, and if it's one thing us Italians value the most, it's the next generation."

"No," Dane states again. "From the beginning, they've made it difficult. Hell, Sal, they threatened you and would have killed you if we hadn't been there. The Donatis can't be trusted. And you know as well as I do money doesn't buy loyalty."

A brief shared look with my men confirms his point. "You're right." With a heavy sigh, I stand. "We all have jobs to do. And as Dane told Dirt, we all need to be discreet."

"We have a plan, and we each know what we need to do. Tomorrow, the fun begins."

The weight of our deliberations still hangs in the air as Dane's firm voice signals the conclusion of our meeting. Like synchronized movement, the men around the round table rise, their chairs scraping softly against the plastic on the barn floor. The creaking wood bears witness to the gravity of the decisions made, each echoing step serving as a somber punctuation mark to our collective contemplation.

Exiting the barn, the cold night air hits us, a stark contrast to the intensity within. Car doors open and shut, the metallic sounds punctuating the night. Headlights flicker to life, casting fleeting beams on the dusty ground as the men disperse into waiting cars. In this moment of departure, the camaraderie and shared burden of responsibility linger.

Once inside the car with Dane and my men, I say, "That went better than I thought it would."

Dane agrees, "Yeah. At least we are all on the same page. Still, the road ahead isn't going to be easy."

The engine hums to life as we pull away from the barn, the gravel crunching beneath the tires. In the dimly lit car, the glow from the dashboard casts shifting shadows on Dane's face, emphasizing the weariness etched in his features. As he maneuvers through the winding paths, the headlights cutting through the darkness, we head toward an uncertain future, and I pray our families survive what's coming.

CHAPTER 11

DIRT

This morning, the weight of last night's meeting hangs heavily on my soul. Since daybreak, I've been up, the rhythmic thud of the axe against wood a feeble attempt to work through the impending turmoil. It's not as though I haven't been in the thick of it over the years, but I know when the MC goes to war, it's the innocents who end up getting hurt.

Lore.

Amidst the swirling thoughts, her name surfaces.

Her face has been a constant presence in my mind since the day I first saw her at the hospital. She claims we lead different lives, and she's not wrong. Yet, as the morning light filters through the trees, I can't shake the notion that if Dane can navigate a relationship with a famous rock star like

Kat, perhaps an old man like me can find a way to make it work with Lore.

The distant hum of a car approaching pulls me away from the repetitive thud of the axe, and I embed it into the wood. Walking to the front of my property, there, navigating the driveway with precision, is Lore's rental car.

As she stops just inches from me, she questions with a smile, "You trust me that much?"

"Guess I figured you wouldn't want to damage the car and have to pay an excess," I respond, a smirk playing on my lips.

Lore giggles. "Maybe?" Stepping out of the vehicle, she stands beside me. "Zeke told me where you live. I hope that's okay?"

"Yeah, it's fine. Can I make you a coffee?"

"Absolutely." Lore reaches out, her fingers lightly tracing the wolf tattoo at the center of my chest. "How come you're all sweaty? It's barely eight o'clock."

"I've been chopping wood." I grab her hand and lead her around the back of my house.

The stacked wood, as tall as the shed it sits beside, is three logs deep and just as high.

Lore surveys the scene. "How long have you been awake?"

"It helps me think," I explain.

Lore glances around. "You have a nice home."

"Yeah, it's quiet out here. Come on, I'll give you

the grand tour inside."

The back door is open, and I kick off my boots in the mudroom before I lead Lore into the house.

"This is the kitchen. I only got it remodeled last year."

Lore touches the light granite countertop. "I like it."

"Kat helped me. I was going for dark everything, but she assured me I wouldn't like a black countertop. She said the dust would show," I explain as we move on. "Dining room."

"Small but very usable," observes Lore.

"Next is the living room, and down here are the bedrooms." I push open the doors as I walk down the hallway. "Bathroom if you need it, but it still needs to be remodeled."

Lore peeks in. "Nice color." She's grinning at me, clearly teasing.

The bathroom has pale green and brown tiles, a vintage feature of the house.

"It's on my to-do list. Maybe next year." We reach the door at the end of the hall—my bedroom. Stepping inside, I gesture around. "This is where I sleep."

Lore walks past me, scanning my room. "Did Kat help you decorate in here too?"

"Why?"

"I can't see you picking out this comforter on your own."

Chuckling, I nod. "It was a present from her for my birthday. But I do like the color."

"Yeah, you always liked blue."

I'm surprised she remembered. "Still do." Putting my hands in my pockets, I ask, "How's Tobias?"

"Much better. He was up and walking yesterday." Lore sits on the end of my bed. "He's so lucky. It could have been so much worse."

I sit beside her, my desire to kiss her overwhelming, yet I don't want to rush the moment. For me, air carries a palpable tension, the unspoken connection between us sparking a delicate dance of emotions.

"How's the weather been treating you lately?" I blurt out, the mundane question a feeble attempt to bridge the gap between desire and restraint.

Lore looks at me and laughs. Her hand cups my cheek, and she leans in, kissing me softly. "Eww!" Lore moves away from me as she giggles. "Go shower, you're all filmy."

Smiling at her, I stand. "I'll just be a minute."

"Take your time. I'll go make us a coffee."

"Do you need any help?"

Lore stands and puts her hand on her hips. "I'll figure it out."

Quickly, I slip into the bathroom, shutting the door behind me, and let my jeans fall to the floor. The aging bathroom has one of those showers over the bath, its curtain a clingy companion that threatens to stick if you venture too close. With swift efficiency, I lather up with soap covering every inch, even my hair, before rinsing off in record time.

Drying off, I drape the towel around my hips and lean over the sink to brush my teeth. When I look at myself in the mirror, my hair is sticking up in all directions. I comb it into submission, attempting to regain some semblance of order, then step out of the bathroom.

In the hallway, uncertainty creeps in.

Do I go into my bedroom and change?

Do I walk out to the kitchen with only a towel wrapped around me?

Hell, I don't even know if Lore is seeing anyone. Maybe this is just a courtesy call?

"Are you okay?"

"Ahh, yeah. I'm going to get dressed."

"Coffee's ready."

"Cool. I'll only be a minute."

Rushing back into my bedroom, I put on a black T-shirt, underwear, and jeans. My hair gets slightly messed, so I run my hands through it before joining Lore in the kitchen. She's sitting naked at the dining table, sipping her coffee, her long brown hair with blonde streaks falling over her shoulders, almost cover her breasts.

"I think I'm over dressed," I quip.

Lore laughs, the sound rich and honeyed. "Just a bit," she agrees, standing and walking toward me with a slow, deliberate grace.

My pulse quickens as she approaches, every inch of her exposed form driving me wild with need.

"Focus," I tell myself, placing one foot in front of the other, closing the distance between us.

Lore stands before me, eyes full of desire and lips parted with anticipation. I run my hands over her body, tracing the curves and valleys. She responds to my touch, melting into my embrace as if we were one.

We move together in harmony, our breathing heavy and our passion rising. We are lost in one another now, all doubts and fears forgotten in the heat of the moment.

Reaching down, I pull my T-shirt over my head, desperate to have her naked form against my own, then I kick off my jeans and underwear.

The outside world slowly fades away until it is just us—two souls joined in perfect union, exploring every inch of each other's bodies with an eagerness bordering on desperation. Our lips meet desperately, no part left untouched or unexplored.

My hands grip her hips to keep our balance as I guide her toward my bedroom. As we cross the threshold, I feel her slender fingers wrap around my erection. She gives a slow, teasing stroke up and down, sending shivers running down my spine. Her touch is like lightning, leaving trails of fire in its wake.

"I've missed you," she whispers.

Our momentum carries us forward, and she falls backward onto the bed, her eyes shimmering with unspoken desire.

Crawling over her, I plant a knee between her thighs and hover above her, drinking in the sight of her flushed cheeks and swollen lips. "Not as much as I've missed you," I reply, my words thick with emotion.

Her fingers trail along my jawline, their touch featherlight as they trace the contours of my face. "I've thought about this moment so many times," she admits, her voice trembling slightly.

As our tongues tangle together, a surge of electricity courses through me, igniting a fire deep within my core. My hands roam her body, and Lore responds with moans of pleasure.

"Every inch of you is perfect," I murmur against her lips, my breath hitching as her hips arch up to meet mine.

My lips find their way to her chest, delicately kissing each nipple in turn. The taste of her skin is intoxicating.

"You're amazing," I breathe out the words against her flushed skin.

Lore moans softly, her fingers entwining in my hair, gently urging me on. It's clear she's missed this connection as much as I have, and the sounds she makes only fuel my desire for her.

As I reach her thighs, I nip and suck along the sensitive inner flesh, relishing in the little gasps and whimpers that escape her. She squirms beneath me, a mixture of anticipation and pleasure etched across her face. I sense her need, and it mirrors my own.

"Please," she whispers, looking at me with pleading eyes.

"Patience, love," I say, smirking slightly.

I spread her legs wider, allowing myself full access to her most intimate area. My heart races as I take in the sight before me—she's beautiful, vulnerable, and completely mine.

Leaning in closer, I run my tongue along her slick folds. Her body shudders in response, and I know I'm hitting all the right spots. And then, I focus on her sensitive nub, swirling my tongue around it, applying just the right amount of pressure.

"Oh God!" Lore cries out, her voice filled with ecstasy.

"Is this what you wanted?" I ask teasingly, pausing for a moment to look up at her.

"Y-yes," she stammers, struggling to catch her breath. "Don't stop."

"Your wish is my command," I say, a playful smirk tugging at my lips.

Lore moans and writhes beneath me, her

pleasure reaching new heights as I continue to drive her wild. With each caress, I feel our connection deepen even further until, finally, it's too much to take.

"Oh my God," Lore cries out, her voice trembling with desire.

My name falls from her lips like a prayer, and I know that she's close to the edge. Her back arches off the bed as she comes undone around me. I don't finish until I've extracted every last quiver from her.

Lore rises on her elbows, a satisfied smile on her lips, and I can't help but mirror it back at her. "That was amazing," she murmurs softly.

"It definitely was," I say in agreement.

Kissing up her body, I gently ease my cock inside her, every inch a moment of ecstasy for me. It seems as if time slows down, allowing me to savor this intimate connection we share. When I'm completely inside her, I pause, giving us both a chance to adjust to the sensation.

I slowly withdraw, feeling the exquisite friction between us, and then thrust back into her hard. She gasps, her eyes wide with surprise and delight. Her legs wrap around my waist, pulling me deeper into her with each powerful thrust. The room seems to disappear around us, leaving only the heat of our skin against one another and the pounding rhythm of our hearts.

"Ah... Dirt..." She moans softly, her voice barely audible above the sound of our heavy breathing. I can feel her tight muscles clenching around me, drawing me in further, making it nearly impossible to maintain my restraint.

"Just let go, Dirt," she urges between gasps. "Make me yours."

"God, Lore," I pant, my control slipping away as the sensations threaten to consume me.

With each thrust, I allow myself to give in to the primal desires that have taken hold, letting them guide my movements as they become more forceful and urgent. I feel her body responding in kind, meeting every push with equal fervor.

"Mine," I growl, the word torn from my throat as our bodies collide with increasing intensity. "You're mine, Lore."

"Yours," she gasps, her eyes wide and shining with a potent mix of emotions—passion, love, and complete surrender. "Always yours, Dirt."

And with those words, I finally allow myself to relinquish what little control remains, embracing the all-consuming pleasure that surges through me. Together, we reach heights neither of us could have ever imagined, lost in a world of our own creation, bound by the unbreakable connection between us.

We spent the whole day in bed.

The intensity of our lovemaking leaving me satisfied and heavy with sleep. Wrapped in each other's arms, Lore tells me about her bar and the little town she lives in. It sounds like she's made a real home there with friends and a grumpy cat called Cosmo. She found him as a kitten in a dumpster at the back of her bar and nurtured him back to health, but fell in love with the crazy furball and kept him.

As we bask in the afterglow, Lore turns to me with a curious expression. "You never settled down with anyone?"

"No. Years ago, I fell in love with a woman, and it nearly broke me when she left. No one else ever measured up. Doesn't mean I was a monk, but no, there wasn't anyone special." Lore shifts to stare into my eyes. "In fact, you're the only female I've shared this bed with. The others, when I feel the need, only happen at the compound." My admission hangs in the air, altering the atmosphere. Unwilling to let the conversation take a somber turn, I ask, "What about you? Anyone special?"

"No. I keep busy with the bar." Lore's eyes drop

to my chest, and she looks at me with lowered lashes. "But I'm no nun, either, Dirt. I don't want you thinking I locked myself up tight."

Chuckling, I lift her head so I can see into her eyes. "It never crossed my mind for a minute that you would. You're a beautiful woman, Lore. I'm not threatened by past lovers, only future ones."

"Only you while I'm here."

"Ditto."

Lore lays back down, and we stay like that until we fall asleep.

The ringing of a cell phone wakes us. Lore groans beside me, rolling over to bury her face in the pillow as I fumble for my phone on the nightstand. With a sleep-fogged brain, I manage to swipe and answer the call.

"What?" I bark into the receiver, my voice hoarse from interrupted slumber.

I can practically hear the hesitation on the other end of the line as they gather themselves.

"Dirt?"

"You called me, didn't you? What's the fucking time?"

"Sorry man, it's Guru. I've been working all night, and I got something. Do you want me to hang up?"

Guru is the MC's computer wizard. He's new to us, transferring in from another chapter, and although he's good with all things technical, his social skills need work.

"I'm awake now. Hit me."

"Okay, so I was going through the bank accounts for the top members of the Vegas MC when I had an idea," Guru says, his voice gaining speed with each word.

"Hang on." Standing, I walk around the bed, kiss Lore, and pick up a pair of jeans.

"Coffee," Lore mumbles without opening her eyes.

"On it." I pull on my jeans, bend and kiss her again, and walk into the kitchen. "I'm back. But Guru, no technical babble, just get to the point."

"Right, sorry." He clears his throat. "Long story short, I found a series of payments going into a bank account."

"Which member?" I ask gruffly, interrupting him.

"Not a member but a woman tied to the club."

"That was smart of them. How the hell did you track who they are seeing?"

"I thought you didn't want any technical babble?"

"Right, right." I hit the button for the coffee machine. "Who's she tied to?"

"Curtis Owen."

Looking up at the ceiling, the name means nothing. "Who the fuck is Curtis Owen?"

"Bulldog, VP in Vegas."

"Good work, Guru."

"T-thanks," Guru stammers, his gratitude palpable. "Sorry again for the early wake-up call."

"Have you told anyone else?"

"You told me to ring you first, so no. Do you want me to tell anyone else?"

"No. Leave it with me."

As I hang up, my thoughts race with the implications of Guru's discovery.

Lives will change, and loyalties will be tested.

I groan and find a couple of mugs in the cupboard. Turning, I come face to face with Lore, the sight of her instantly calming the turmoil inside me. My hand instinctively reaches out to tuck a stray lock of hair behind her ear.

"You should have stayed in bed."

"It sounded important. Is everything okay?"

The coffee machine beeps, and I get busy making coffee. Lore clad in one of my old T-shirts looks sexy as hell. She sits at the dining table, watching me work.

"You didn't answer my question."

Frowning, I pick up the cups and sit next to her. "Club business."

Lore holds her hands up. "Who am I going to

tell?" I shake my head at her as sharing club business isn't something I've ever done. "Is it bad?" Lore asks.

"Yeah."

A subtle tension settles over her. The lines around her eyes tighten, and her brows furrow ever so slightly. Lore's lips, once at ease, now press together, forming a thin line. The unease in her gaze becomes apparent as she averts her eyes. With a gentle touch, I place a finger under her chin, lifting her gaze to meet mine.

"What are you thinking?" I ask, wanting to know but also worried about what she's about to say.

Lore smiles, but it's one that doesn't reach her eyes. She picks up her coffee cup and takes a sip. Her hand closes around mine, and she lightly shakes her head.

"The not knowing is worse than knowing. Club life and all their secrets were never for me. I want a partnership. I want to come home and bitch and complain about my employees, the shitty customers, or the fact it rained all day, and no one came in." Lore pauses, and once again, I lose her eyes. They are focused on the table, where our hands are locked together. "I can't have that with you, not while you're in the Savage Angels."

It feels like a blow to my chest, knocking the breath from my lungs. My grip on her hand reflexively tightens as if I could hold onto her through sheer force of will. But she is slipping away, and there is nothing I can do to stop it.

Forcing out a laugh, I pat her hand. "This wasn't going to be a long-term thing, Lore. When Tobias is out of the woods, you'll go home, and I'll stay here. Can't we, for now, just have this? Just you and me, having fun, enjoying each other and being in the moment?"

Lore takes a moment, her gaze shifting from my eyes to the intertwined hands resting on the table.

"I know," she finally whispers, a hint of sadness in her voice. "It's just hard not to get attached."

Lore's admission is like a strike to my heart. Never in my wildest dreams did I think she'd want to pursue a real relationship with me. A fling, at best, was all I had dared hope for, but now the possibility of something more lingers in the air.

"You could stay," the words tumble from my lips.

But she shakes her head. "No, I can't. The MC life isn't for me... never really was."

"Right." I nod. "But we have right now, yeah?"

Lore bites her lip, hesitating for a moment before she says, "Yeah, we can."

Yet, in that moment, a subtle shift occurs. I sense the reluctance in her response, a hint of distance that wasn't there before. It's as if a fracture has occurred, and though she's agreeing to be with me, I feel the undertow of her emotions pulling her away. In her eyes, I read a truth she hasn't voiced—

Lore has already made up her mind, and this night we shared now carries an expiration date.

CHAPTER
12

LORE

Walking into Tobias' room at the hospital, I'm stunned to see Mel Carter holding his hand and talking quietly with him. It's been years since I've seen her—she broke his heart when she left. When she sees me, she stands, and I notice she's lost a lot of weight and is perhaps a little too thin. Her once wild hair is tamed into long, black, loose curls held back on one side with a bejeweled comb.

"Lore, how are you?"

She was always polite, and I know she loved my son. After my exchange with Dirt, I now understand why Mel couldn't stay. She hated his lifestyle. Mel didn't like him being around the strip clubs and the MC, mirroring how I feel about Dirt now.

"I'm good." I point at Tobias. "Except for the

heart attack this one is trying to give me. How about you? You look great."

"Told you," Tobias agrees with a smirk.

Mel blushes and waves a hand in his face. "Shut up." She moves around the bed and hugs me. "I'm good too."

"Still working for the church?"

Mel pulls away from me, shaking her head. "No, not for some time. I went private."

"More money?"

She blushes again and walks back to her chair. "Yes." Mel shakes her head. "I got sick of eating packet noodles and always counting my pennies."

Holding up my hands, I say, "No judgment here. You can always go back to it if you feel like you've sold out."

"Mom!"

Arching an eyebrow at Tobias, I say, "What?"

"There's nothing wrong with wanting to earn a little cash and getting ahead."

Frowning, I sit in the chair on the opposite side of his bed. "I never said there was."

"Tobias, it's okay," Mel chimes in, offering a reassuring smile. "It wasn't an easy decision, but I still do the occasional job for the church for free."

Looking at her hand, I ask, "You never married?"

Mel shifts in her seat and glances at Tobias. She hesitates for a moment, her eyes betraying a hint of vulnerability. "No," she finally says, tucking a strand of hair behind her ear. "I came close, but..." her words trail off.

"Mom, you're doing your thing."

"My thing?"

"The thing you do when you're being too personal and making people uncomfortable," Tobias chides, a hint of exasperation evident in his tone.

"Pfft! Don't be ridiculous. Mel is a good-looking woman. I'm just surprised no one else has figured that out."

Tobias glares at me. "*You've* never been married."

Behind me someone clears their throat, and I turn around to see Brooks and a woman, presumably Elizabeth, clutching his hand. "Are we interrupting?"

"Not at all." I stand. "I was just about to go downstairs and get a coffee."

"I'll join you," Mel says as she pats Tobias' hand. "Can I get you anything?"

"You're coming back?"

Mel smiles down at him. "Of course."

He clears his throat. "Good. And no, I'm fine."

"Tobias, aren't you going to introduce us?" Brooks asks.

"Sorry." He shakes his head. "Dad, Elizabeth, this is Mel Carter. Mom, this is Elizabeth, Dad's wife."

Mel shakes hands with the pair while I study

Brooks' wife. She's at least fifteen years younger than him and bears more than a striking resemblance to me.

Holding up my hand, I give her a wave. "Nice to meet you. Can I get you anything from the cafeteria?"

"It's nice to *finally* meet you too, and no, thank you," Elizabeth replies.

She might look like me, but Elizabeth has none of my spunk. With a curt nod, I head for the elevators with Mel following close behind.

"You've never met her before?"

"No, and now I know why." I cast a glance at Mel. "She's a younger version of me, don't you think?"

"He certainly has a type." The doors to the elevator open. "You look good, Lore. Whatever you're doing, keep doing it."

"Thanks, Mel. I meant what I said... y*ou* look good too."

"Lots of hard work and not eating copious amounts of chocolate."

Chuckling, I say, "Sometimes we need chocolate."

Mel grins. "I didn't say I'd given it up. I just don't eat it with every meal anymore."

The doors open, and we walk into the cafeteria. We both order a coffee, and I sit at a table.

"You're not going back up?"

"I'm giving Brooks and Elizabeth some alone time with Tobias." Mel frowns at me. "Brooks isn't good when I'm in the room. He seems determined to start a fight, and I don't want Tobias seeing or feeling it. He needs to concentrate on himself."

Mel sits. "The doctors seem very happy with his progress."

"My boy is a fighter."

She sips her coffee and says, "He gets that from you."

Staring at the steam rising from my coffee, I say, "I just want him to have the best chance at a full recovery." Leaning back in my seat, I ask, "Has he said anything about losing his eye?"

"Apart from pirate jokes and doing a very bad impersonation of Johnny Depp? Not really. I think he's more upset about his hair."

Laughter bubbles out of me. "That's good. That makes me happy. He's never been particularly vain, but he's an attractive man. I was worried it might upset him."

"No." Mel smiles down at the table. "He's remarkable." Her eyes meet mine. "Always was. I've never met a man like him. Tobias doesn't dwell on the bad, only the good. He would have made a good psychiatrist or counselor."

"Being cooped up in an office all day was never going to satisfy him. He loves working at the clubs."

Her smile falters, and she takes another sip of her coffee. "Yeah."

"You know, you 're the only girl he ever

introduced me to?"

Mel spits out her coffee. "What?"

"It's true. I've met some of the girls he works with. They all adore him, but you're the only girl he ever took to my bar."

Mel stands. "I'm going back up."

"Tell Brooks to come find me when he's done. I'll be here."

Mel gives me a small smile and hurries away. I'm guessing she didn't know Tobias hasn't introduced me to any of his girlfriends. He's had plenty over the years, but they were never worthy of meeting me.

A gasp escapes the woman sitting at a table near me, prompting me to follow her wide-eyed stare. In the cafeteria queue, Dane Reynolds looms at six foot six, a towering figure with muscles that seem to stretch for days. His black T-shirt clings so snugly to his frame that I wonder how he manages to breathe. Our eyes lock, and he acknowledges me with a casual two-fingered wave. I return his gesture, pull out my cell phone, and pretend I'm engrossed in something on the screen. In truth, I only use the damn thing as a phone. I don't play games and loathe social media.

Dane strides over. "Can I join you?" Before I answer, he settles into the seat across from me.

"Seems like you have."

"Come on, Lore. We were friendly once."

"That was a long time ago."

"Seems like you've fallen back into old habits. How's Dirt?" he inquires, casually unscrewing the cap of his water bottle and taking a sip.

"Did he tell you?" I ask, suddenly annoyed.

"No. Tourmaline is a small town, and people gossip." He takes another sip from his bottle. "How's Tobias?" His sudden change of topic throws me for a moment.

"Good. Mel's here," I blurt out.

"The counselor?" Dane grins. "He had a soft spot for her. I half expected him to chase after her a while back. Did you ring her?"

"No. Dirt did."

"She's a good match for him."

"Like me, she hates the lifestyle, so maybe not."

Dane frowns. "Tobias is like Dirt. It's what he knows, and Tobias is very good at what he does. *Just like Dirt.*"

I scoff. "It's easy for you. Isn't it, Dane? You send the men in your MC out to do your dirty work while you stay behind, all safe and sound. What about their families? Don't you think they worry about their sons, husbands, or fathers?"

Dane takes a deep breath, his chest expanding as he inhales, then slowly releases the air through slightly parted lips. "The MC you knew isn't the MC we have today."

"Right, so my son got shot for jaywalking?" The sarcasm drips from my words like venom.

He meets my gaze, his eyes steady and unflinching. "Lore, I told you we had nothing to do with that."

"Right, so you're telling me you're all choir boys now? No more drugs, no more gun running, no more whores?"

"That's right, except for the whores, but it's not what you think."

"What?"

"It hasn't been easy changing the way things have always been done. I've been trying to show my men there's another path… one that doesn't involve violence, bloodshed, and fighting for territory," he pauses. "The women are there by choice. They have the opportunity to earn decent money, but they aren't the whores you remember. No one is strung out or pressured to do anything."

"Wait, you pulled the MC out of guns and drugs?" I say in disbelief.

"Not all chapters, but I'm working on it. It's too easy for my men to get hooked, and then it makes it simple for the law to flip them. I've visited enough of my brothers in jail that I don't want to do it anymore."

Studying his face, I search for any hint of deception, any sign he is lying to me. But all I see is sincerity or at least a convincing reproduction of it. My mind races, torn between wanting to believe him and fearing this is just a lie.

"How long have you been working toward this?"

"Since the day I became president. It's been hard. Some of the other chapters only have drugs, guns, and whores... it's easy money. Convincing them to invest in garages, strip clubs, tattoo parlors, and real estate sounds a lot like selling out to them. But things are changing, and Tobias is part of the change."

"You expect me to believe you?"

The corner of his mouth lifts into a wry smile. "I wouldn't expect you to, Lore. Talk to Dirt... he'll tell you everything."

Astounded at his confession, I cross my arms over my chest and scrutinize him. The man before me was not the reckless, cold-hearted leader I had known all those years ago. This Dane is different and seems determined to pull his MC out of the dark ages.

"I'm going up to visit with Tobias."

Shaking my head, I say, "His father is up there visiting. Give them some time alone."

"Is it cool if I sit with you?"

"It's a free country."

"Do you think you'll make a go of it with Dirt?"

My brows come together, and I give him a small smile. "Even with all the changes you say you've made, Dirt would stand beside you if you needed him to. I need a man to stand next to me, and he can't do that."

Dane considers my words for a moment, his expression thoughtful. "Maybe Dirt could leave the MC." His gaze is distant. "If it came down to it, and he had to choose between the club and you, maybe he'd walk away."

I raise an eyebrow at his words.

Dane leans back in his chair, crossing his arms. "I've seen men make choices they never thought they would. Love has a way of shifting priorities."

I glance away, contemplating the possibility. "But even if he did, what about you, Dane? Would you let him leave?"

He meets my eyes with a solemn expression. "I don't want anyone in my MC who doesn't want to be there, Lore."

I nod, acknowledging the complexity of his struggle. Despite my reservations, there's a glimmer of hope that maybe people can change, and perhaps the man sitting across from me is genuinely striving for a different path.

"Would you ever leave?"

Dane barks out a laugh. "No. I'm a lifer. Tourmaline is my home. I couldn't leave the MC in someone else's hands and watch them revert to the old ways. You and I know the lure of easy money for some is better than working hard." He taps the table. "I can tell you don't believe most of what I've said about the MC changing. It's the same for some of the members. It's what they've always done, so why change?" He sighs. "I'm not saying we aren't still on the fringes of society, but some of us can blend in now and are almost respectable."

"Getting married changed you," I state.

There's a quiet strength in the set of his jaw and the steadiness of his gaze. "No. I was on this path before Kat came into my life. Being one step ahead of the law and keeping her and my MC safe from past and present dangers, whether that's rival MC or the law, is all I think about."

"Money?"

Dane chuckles. "And money. Yep, that's a priority too.."

Brooks appears in front of me. "Tobias is asking for you."

Dane and I both rise to our feet. "Brooks, this is Dane. Dane, this is Tobias' father, Brooks."

Brooks looks up at Dane and holds out his hand. "Are you a friend of my son's?"

"More like family."

They shake, and Brooks tilts his head to the side, scrutinizing Dane. "You're part of that MC, aren't you?"

"Not just a part." Dane nods at me. "See you up there."

Brooks watches him go, his face turning red. "How can you let him visit Tobias?"

I laugh. "Oh, honey, you don't *let* Dane Reynolds do anything. He just does."

"You know it's all your fault? If you hadn't fallen in with this MC, Tobias would *never* have gone looking for them." He throws both hands in the air. "The way you used to talk about your life here, it's a wonder Tobias never joined them."

Staggering back a step at his words, I can feel my anger rising.

"You were trash then, and you're trash now."

"Fuck *you*," I growl out at him in a hiss. "You were a good father to our son, and I thank you for that. But this *isn't* on me. Tobias is a grown-assed man."

"Lore—"

"No, you shut your fucking mouth." I poke him in the chest. "You come here all high and mighty with your wife, who looks like a carbon copy of me, only younger." I poke him again. "Well, I've had enough. I've tried to keep the peace all these years, but Brooks, I never loved you. You were a mistake that resulted in the best damn thing I ever did in my life. But you and I... we were never going to work. Oil and water don't mix, and you and I are the same. I'm done being nice to you!" My voice rises. "I'm done letting you talk down to me. I'm done with your continued attempts to win me back. And I'm done letting Tobias think you're a fucking saint!"

A sharp gasp echoes behind me, and I turn to find Elizabeth standing there, holding two cups of coffee. My lips tighten into a firm line as I catch the expression on Brooks' face when he notices her. His eyes flicker between Elizabeth and me.

"Go be with your *wife*," I spit out, my words carrying a harshness I've never used to talk to him. I walk out of the cafeteria and toward the elevators.

"I'm not done talking to you!"

The elevator doors open, and I step inside.

Brooks is charging toward me, frustration etched on his face.

In response, I defiantly hold up my middle finger and offer a sardonic smile as the doors close. The hum of the elevator takes me back to Tobias, but it does nothing to calm my anger. For years, I've put up with Brooks. He was a good father to Tobias, but I'm done pretending he was ever good to me.

The doors open, and I see Dane in the waiting room talking to one of his men. I give them a curt nod, and I continue toward Tobias' room. Mel is back in her chair, and they are talking quietly. Whatever she sees on my face causes her to rise.

"Lore, are you okay?"

"Yes. No. I will be."

"Did you and Dad finally have it out?" Tobias asks.

"What?"

"It's okay, Mom. I know what he's like."

Collapsing into a nearby chair, I say, "You knew?"

"I'm a good study of the human race. It's obvious Dad never got over you. Elizabeth is a testament to that."

With my head in my hands, I mumble, "She looks like me."

"Yeah, she does, but not in spirit. Elizabeth doesn't have your backbone, and she does whatever Dad wants."

"Why didn't you tell me he was getting married?"

Tobias shrugs. "I knew you wouldn't care. You moved on from Dad a long time ago."

Brooks strides into the room. "You bitch!" Spittle flies from his lips.

"Dad, calm down."

Dirt and Dane walk in. They each take one of Brooks' arms and walk him backward out of the room without uttering a word.

"Don't hurt him!" yells Tobias.

"They won't." I stand and walk to the doorway and stop to look at my son. He's holding hands with Mel. "I'll handle your father. You need to focus on yourself, on getting better."

He glances at me, a mix of concern and gratitude in his eyes. "But, Mom—"

"No buts," I interrupt gently. "I've dealt with your father's tantrums before. It's time I put an end to them for good. You've got more important things to worry about right now." Mel squeezes Tobias' hand reassuringly, and I shoot him a supportive smile. "You just focus on healing."

As I turn to leave, I catch a glimpse of Dirt and Dane outside the room, ensuring Brooks stays away. With a determined stride, I head toward Brooks, ready to confront the storm he's brewing.

"Outside," I state as I hit the button for the elevator.

"I will not be told—"

Dane grabs Brooks by his shirt collar, lifts him, and throws him through the elevator doors. "Sort out your shit with Lore, or you don't get to come back and visit with your son."

"I'll call the police!"

Dane smirks. "Yeah, you go ahead and do that. Tell them Dane Reynolds and the Savage Angels say hello."

Dirt stands beside me as the doors close, trapping all three of us inside.

Brooks' nostrils flare as he looks at Dirt. "Why is *he* here?"

Dirt quirks an eyebrow. "I'm here in case the lady needs protecting." He looks Brooks up and down. "But I'm pretty sure she can take you. You're nothing special."

A vein begins to pulse at Brooks' temple, and his face turns red. The elevator announces we are on the ground floor, and he walks out, headed for the hospital's exit.

Rushing to keep up with him, I grab his arm when we're outside, and he abruptly turns toward me.

"What? What do you want, Lore?"

"For starters, how about you calm the fuck down?"

He steps back, shaking his head. "You poison everything you touch."

"Brooks, what's going on? Why are you behaving this way?"

Elizabeth stands next to me. "It's my fault."

Brooks points at her. "Don't."

Confused, I glance from one to the other.

"I'm not her." Elizabeth's voice holds a forcefulness to it. "I know you were attracted to me because I look like her, but I'm not Lore. I won't leave. *I love you.* Can't you see that?"

The anger seems to drain out of him as he stares at his wife. "I'm too old."

"You're not," Elizabeth states.

"Too old for what?" I ask, confused.

Elizabeth, with her eyes on Brooks, says, "I'm pregnant."

Brooks' shoulders sag. "I can't raise another child on my own."

She holds up her hand and points to her wedding ring. "Married, remember? I'm not going anywhere. You once told me this meant I was bought and paid for. Well, that goes for you too."

Suddenly feeling like a third wheel, I walk back into the hospital where Dirt is waiting.

"Is everything okay?" Dirt reaches for my hand.

"She pregnant. It's why he's been more of a prick

than usual. A blind man can tell she looks like me but *isn't* me. Seems like Brooks is scared he's going to be a single dad all over again."

"Tobias turned out okay."

"Yeah, he did. He's the best of us."

With a tug on my hand, Dirt takes me back to Tobias.

Dane is standing at the foot of his bed, and they're laughing.

When Tobias sees me, the laughter stops. "Is Dad okay?"

"Yes and no. You're going to have a brother or a sister."

"*You're* pregnant?" Tobias exclaims.

"No. Elizabeth is. Jesus, son, I'm too old for that."

Dane laughs. "I read a thing the other day where a woman in her seventies gave birth to twins."

Quickly, I hold up my hands. "No way, no how!"

"Was I that bad?"

Reaching out, I put my hand on his chest. "No, honey, you were and are perfect, so why strive for another when I already have the best possible son in front of me." Dane feigns gagging, and Dirt bursts into laughter. "Oh, shut up, you two."

"You've gotta admit it was pretty soppy, Mom."

"Pfft! It's the truth."

Brooks and Elizabeth didn't come back inside the hospital. Dirt, Dane, and I visited with Tobias for another half an hour and left. It was easy to see he wanted to spend time alone with Mel, and the two men clearly had something they needed to get to. Dirt kept checking the clock on the wall.

Now, I'm at my hotel, drinking a soda, sitting on the bed with my back against the headboard, channel surfing. My cell phone rings and the screen reads *Dean*.

"Did my bar burn down?" I tease.

Dean's laughter rumbles down the line. "Not yet, although we did have a nasty surprise in the toilets last night. I'm going to need danger money from now on."

Laughing, I ask, "We could look at it. What can I do for you?"

"Not that I don't mind looking after the place, but I was wondering when you're coming home?"

"Aww, do you miss me?"

"Always." He chuckles. "Ahh, shit, I haven't even asked about your son."

"He's awake, doing good." I smile into the cell phone. "The doctor says he's going to make a full recovery, minus an eye."

"I'm glad. So... are you leaving soon?"

"Got a hot date?" Dean goes quiet. "Dean?"

"Lore, I know in the past we have been... friendly, but I've met someone."

"Me too. Well, an old someone. So, who's the lucky girl?"

"Don't freak out."

I groan. "Jesus, tell me it isn't someone from the bar?"

"What? No!" He laughs. "Cosmo broke into the pantry and munched on a few packet sauce mixes. He's fine. His mouth got infected, and he looked like a chipmunk, but he's getting better every day," he finishes quickly.

"How on earth did he get into the pantry?"

"I may have left the door open," Dean confesses.

"Dean!"

"Hey, he's fine. And that's where I met Alice. She's the vet who treated him."

"Did you at least get a discount?"

"Not really. I used some of the money out of your cookie jar."

The cookie jar is where I keep excess cash the government doesn't need to know about, and I use it for rainy days. Dean has been in my home more than once, so he knows it's there.

"Thanks, Dean. So, you're serious about this one?"

"Yeah. What about you?"

Exhaling, I pick up the remote and turn off the television. "I don't know. It's complicated, and we have history."

"It's not Brooks, is it?"

Laughing, I say, "God, no! His name is Dirt."

"Dirt?"

"Yeah, as in if you mess with me, I'll punch you, and your teeth will wind up in the dirt."

"Ahh, he sounds nice," Dean teases.

Holding the cell phone to my ear, I nod. "He is, but he's in the Savage Angels."

"The MC? Damn, Lore, I thought you didn't date bikers?"

"He's an old flame." I put my feet on the floor and stand. "Can you give me one more week?"

"I can do that. Thanks, Lore."

"Thank you for looking after things. I'm not sure what I would have done if you hadn't stepped up."

I hear his intake of breath. "So, we're cool?"

"I'm utterly heartbroken, but yeah," I reply with a smile in my voice.

Moving through the motel, I open the curtains to find Dirt standing on the other side.

Dean chuckles, and in my mind, I can see him shaking his head at me. "And Lore, you said it was complicated? Uncomplicate it. You deserve to be happy."

"Thanks, Dean. Talk soon."

I end the call, open the door, and smile at Dirt. "You stalking me, biker?"

"Could be, if you're into that sort of thing?"

Holding the door wide open, I grin at him. "Come on in."

"You were on the phone. I hope I wasn't interrupting?"

"It was work. Dean, who's looking after things, wanted to know when I'll be going back."

Dirt's face twists into a scowl. "Ahh, right. So, what did you tell him?"

"In a week."

His chin goes up, and he runs a hand through his hair. "I thought we'd have more time."

"Tobias is doing well. The doc said he would be starting physical therapy tomorrow. There's no need for me to stay."

Dirt's eyebrows both shoot up. "Maybe I want you to stay?"

Putting both hands on his face, I move in closer. "We agreed this was temporary, remember?"

"Yeah, but a week isn't long enough. I need more time with you, Lore."

"You could come with me? See Willowbrook Falls through my eyes."

Dirt pulls me close and kisses me as his lips meet mine. There's a soft brush and a tentative exploration that ignites a spark within me. The kiss deepens, his hands find the small of my back, pulling me in, and slowly our troubles and the outside world fade away. This pull I feel for Dirt intensifies as we kiss. Our breaths become ragged, and the very air around us seems charged with electricity. Every touch sends a shiver through me, and I know I'm lost to him.

Reaching down, I tug at his belt while he kicks out of his boots. His jeans hit the floor with a thud. Dirt's fingers fumble with the button of my jeans and zipper. When he finally gets them open, I shimmy out of them, and he cups my sex.

First, one finger, then two enter me. "So, fucking tight," he murmurs between kisses.

"I need you."

"Not yet."

I drop to my knees and swirl my tongue around the tip of his cock. A sharp intake of breath escapes him, and then his hands are in my hair, guiding me up and down his hard penis.

"Jesus, Lore," he cries out.

Remembering he used to like it when I made a noise, I hum, and he quickens his pace. Cupping his balls in my hand, Dirt moans long and loud but abruptly pulls me to my feet, turns me around, and pushes me onto the bed.

This is what I wanted.

I rise on my knees, and he pounds into me. His fingers find my nub, and he teases me.

"Oh, yes!"

"Is this what you wanted?"

"Yes, Dirt. Don't stop!"

His cock hits just the right spot, and with the added pressure on my clit, the familiar tingle spreads through me.

"I'm coming," I whisper.

"That's my girl." He grunts as he moves in and out of me at a punishing speed.

My pussy contracts, and he groans loudly. His cock is a perfect fit as he moves in and out. Clutching the comforter, I match his speed as another wave of pleasure surges through me, so much more intense than the first.

"Lore," Dirt cries out as he plants himself deep within me.

When he's done, Dirt pulls out and falls on the bed beside me. "I'm sorry that was quick."

With a smirk, I say, "It's what I wanted. A quick end to a very long day."

Dirt touches my face. "I aim to please."

"We were always good at this."

He stares into my eyes. "Yeah, it's the other stuff we suck at."

"Stuff?"

"Talking. Keeping it real. Lore, I'm willing to try if you are."

Shaking my head, I move in and kiss his lips. "Not tonight. Let's order pizza or Chinese, watch TV, and not think."

"Lore—"

I put a finger to his lips. "Can't we just have tonight?"

Dirt nods, but I know he wants to have a deeper conversation.

One I'm simply not ready to have.

CHAPTER
13

LORE

The sterile smell of antiseptic fills my nostrils as I step into the pristine white hallway of the Baptist Hospital. In the short time I've been here, I've become all too familiar with these walls as I make my way to Tobias' room.

"Good morning, Mrs. Mercer," greets Dr. Grills. She's a tall, slender woman with salt and pepper hair and a pair of wire-rimmed glasses perched on her nose. "How are you today?"

"Morning, Doc," I reply, forcing a small smile. "I'm doing all right, thanks. How's Tobias coming along?"

"Remarkably well, considering his injuries," Dr. Grills says, eyes scanning over the clipboard in her hands. "He's been working hard with our physical therapists, and his determination is truly inspiring."

"I'm on my way to see him."

"Of course, he's expecting you." Dr. Grills gestures toward Tobias' room before excusing herself.

Pushing open the door, I find Tobias in the middle of a physical therapy session. Sweat beads on his forehead as he strains to lift a modestly weighted dumbbell, his face etched with fierce determination.

"Hey, Mom," he says through gritted teeth, his voice shaking from the effort.

"Hey, sweetheart. You're doing great."

"Thanks," Tobias huffs, dropping the weights and wiping his brow.

"What did Dr. Grills have to say?"

"She told me every injury is different and follows its own timeline, but because I'm doing so well, I might be able to go home sooner rather than later."

The idea of him rushing to get home bothers me as he lives by himself.

"Tobias, don't rush it. Give yourself time to heal."

"I hate hospitals," he admits. "And they wake you up all night and ask you your name and date of birth. It's annoying." He reaches out, and I put my hand in his. "You have a business you need to get back to, and Cosmo must be missing you."

Tilting my head from side to side, I say, "Yeah,

especially after his visit to the vet."

"What happened?"

"Dean is looking after him, and he left the pantry open. Cosmo helped himself to sauce packet mixes." Tobias gives me a confused look. "You know, the ones you use to make gravy or a bearnaise sauce."

"I thought you did everything from scratch?" he teases.

"Yeah, right." Tentatively, I touch his head. "How are we feeling about losing your... hair?"

Tobias reaches up and touches the bandage over his head. "Lucky. It'll grow back unlike other things."

"Is it strange?"

"My depth perception is for shit at the moment." He lets go of my hand and rises. "Doc said it should improve over time. She also said I've only actually lost twenty percent of my vision, and over time, I'll compensate for that by turning my head without even realizing it."

"So not so bad, after all?"

Tobias puts his hands on his hips. "I'd prefer to have both my eyes, but yeah, it's better than being dead." Immediately, I move in and put my arms around his waist. Tobias hugs me close. "Hey, Mom, I'm okay."

"I nearly lost you."

He pulls back slightly, looking into my eyes with

a reassuring smile. "But you didn't. I'm here, and I'm going to be okay. I promise." After a pause, he glances around the room. "So, tell me more about Cosmo's culinary adventure with the sauce mixes. I could use a good laugh."

"Dean said his cheeks swelled up like a chipmunk."

Tobias laughs, the sound filling the room. "That cat is something else. I'm looking forward to going home and then visiting you both."

His mention of going home tugs at my heart. "Are you sure you're ready for that, Tobias? I don't want you pushing yourself too hard."

He nods, a determined glint in his eyes. "I'll take it easy, Mom, I promise. But being in my own space, surrounded by familiar things, that's a part of my healing too."

Tobias will always be my son, and even though he's a man now, I still worry, and the thought of him at home alone makes me a bit anxious. "Just promise me you'll listen to your body and not overdo it."

"I promise," he says sincerely.

Mel walks in, a huge smile on her face. "Did you do your exercises without me?"

"Mom watched."

"For about five seconds. Were you supposed to have supervision?"

Tobias walks back to his bed and sits on it. "I *did*

have supervision. They left, and I kept going for a bit."

"Were you supposed to?" I ask, hands on my hips.

"Yes. It's all about recovery."

Mel moves to stand near him, and he reaches out to touch her. "You're doing great. Don't overdo it."

He flicks his head in my direction. "Now you sound like her."

Mel laughs. "Maybe that's not such a bad thing."

He lets her go and positions himself back in bed. "I wasn't expecting you to come in today. I thought you had to work?"

"Good unexpected or bad unexpected?" Mel asks.

"Good unexpected," he assures her. "Definitely good."

Mel sits in the chair nearest his bed, and he again reaches for her, and they hold hands. It's a small gesture, but it's so intimate, and I feel as though I'm intruding on their time together.

"I should go."

Tobias' head swivels in my direction. "You just got here."

"Yeah, but I have stuff to do."

Tobias holds up their joined hands. "Mom, you're not interrupting anything. I'm in a hospital, for God's sake."

"Tobias!" Mel shrieks.

Laughing, I pull out a chair and sit. "Fine, I'll stay

for a while."

Mel stands, her face a pretty shade of red. "I need a soda. Do either of you want anything?"

"Coffee, black," I say.

"Something sweet? A cake or a brownie or a cookie?"

Mel nods. "I'll be back in a minute."

When she's out of the room, I say, "What happened to... my body is my temple and all that crap?"

"You try surviving on hospital food." Tobias chuckles.

It's good to see he hasn't lost his sense of humor. "Want me to bring you in a home-cooked meal?"

He raises an eyebrow. "How? When you're staying in a motel? Why didn't you stay at my place?"

"Because it's *your* place, and you weren't awake to ask."

"My home is your home, Mom. You never need to ask."

"The motel is fine, and it's closer than your apartment."

"My apartment is *free*."

"I'll think about it."

He closes his eye and rests his head back. "How's Dirt?"

"Are you tired?"

He shakes his head but doesn't open his eye.

"Sometimes it throbs a little. Closing my eyes..." he pauses, "... eye... helps. And how's Dirt?"

"Have you told the doctor? Do you need me to call someone?"

Tobias rolls his head to the side and looks at me. "No and no. Now answer my question."

"He's good."

"Rumor has it you two are reconnecting." He makes air quotes with his fingers.

"Who told you that?"

"Mom, Tourmaline is a small town, and a couple of the girls who work for me told me."

"When did you see them?"

He rolls his one good eye to the ceiling and says, "They come in late after their shifts. Apparently, you told everyone to stay away. They make sure no one is here and visit. The nurses let them in, even if it's two in the morning."

"You should be sleeping."

"I've worked nights for years, Mom. Sleeping through the day is my normal."

Frowning, I admit, "I hadn't thought of that."

"It's cool. They all think you're a bitch." He closes his eye and smiles. "Of course, I told them you're not."

"Why don't I believe you?"

He chuckles and holds up his hands in surrender. "So, Dirt?"

Sighing, I lean back in the chair. "The reason we

split up years ago was because of the MC, and he's still in the MC. I can't see us working out."

"You really like him, don't you?"

Looking down at my hands, I say, "Yeah. He's the one who got away. But I can't be worried every time he goes out on a ride with them. It's no way to live."

"The MC isn't what it used to be."

Scoffing, I say, "Now you sound like Dane."

"Why do you think I got involved with them in the first place? Dane is forcing change upon them, and he's pulled them out of a lot of shit. They *aren't* what you remember." Not wanting to argue with him, I remain silent. Tobias looks at me. "Do you care for him?"

"Yes," I answer honestly.

He smiles. "Years ago, a woman I know gave me some words of wisdom. She told me to always follow my heart and do the right thing."

I laugh. "Do *not* throw my half-assed psychiatry at me."

"It's good advice."

"He lives here, and I live in Willowbrook Falls. It can't work."

"If you truly care about him, you'll find a way."

Waving a hand in the air, I say, "I don't want to have to deal with the MC."

"Pretty sure they don't allow women in their ranks, so you're good."

Mel walks back in and hands me a cup of coffee.

I stand. "Thanks. I'm going to leave you two alone."

"Mom—"

Holding up a hand, I say, "Last time I checked, my love life was none of your business."

Mel hands him a small brown paper bag. "Oh, what did I miss?"

"Mom is seeing Dirt."

"Really?"

"No comment." I place my purse on my shoulder. "Take care of him, Mel, and if you need anything, give me a call."

"Mom, you're being—"

Holding up my hand, I press my thumb and two fingers together and say, "Zip it! End of conversation." I bend and kiss his forehead. "See you tomorrow."

CHAPTER 14

DIRT

Dane sits at the head of the table with Jonas on one side and me on the other. King is at the far end, strumming his fingers on the wooden surface as we wait for Sal to join us. At first, he was surprised we'd allow Sal into this space, but now he only seems agitated at having to wait on the man.

My phone buzzes with a text message.

Lore: *Good morning!*

The text is followed by a winky face, a kiss, and an eggplant emoji.

I bark out a laugh, and Dane looks at me.

"Lore," I say by way of an explanation.

He nods, a smirk on his lips. "How is she?"

"Good."

Jonas chuckles. "From the smile on your face, I'd say better than good."

"Is that the old chick I saw you having breakfast with the other day?" King asks.

"She's not old, and yeah."

He leans forward, elbows resting on the table. "Hey, I'm not saying she wasn't hot, but I like mine a little younger. Although they say a woman with experience is better." He leans back and raps his knuckles on the table. "So long as you're getting your dick dipped, it doesn't really matter, does it?"

Ignoring him, I twist in my seat and stare at the wall.

"Aww, come on, Dirt. I'm only fucking with you."

"Why are you here?" I ask him without moving.

"*Dirt*," Dane says in a stern tone.

"What do you mean?"

I turn to stare at him.

"Dirt, let it go," orders Dane.

King stands and leans over the table. "Let him speak. Have you got something to say, Dirt?"

Standing, I point at him. "You're a fucking disgrace. You come in here and challenge Dane at every opportunity when your own chapter is a fucking mess."

King strides toward me, and although he's taller than me, I stand and face him. He's so close our chests are touching.

"What did you say?"

"You fucking heard me."

He raises his fist and swings. I block it and hit him hard in the kidneys. King growls and swings again, hitting me in the jaw and sending me flying backward. Quickly, I get to my feet and charge, grabbing him around the waist, then lifting him up and throwing him down hard onto the wooden floors.

"Get up, you bastard, and we'll see what you're made of," I sneer at him.

"For fuck's sake, *enough*!" bellows Dane.

King scrambles to his feet, and we circle each other, fists raised. He throws the first punch, and I dodge it. King throws a second punch, and I dodge that too. He moves his left shoulder before he executes a punch so I know what's coming. A good fighter gives nothing away, and I earned my name by being able to read the signs of a bad fighter. The key is to keep out of reach and hit them hard and fast, especially when they have size and bulk on them like King does on me.

"Are we going to dance or do this?" he torments me.

Dane moves in between us. "I will *not* have this shit in my house."

Dropping my fists, I stare daggers at King, whose face is so red he looks about ready to have a stroke.

"This isn't over, *Dirt*," he sneers.

"Anytime, anywhere, you just name the place."

"Dirt, sit the fuck down before I put you down," Dane orders. "And you? This is *my* house, and you respect *my* rules."

"I'm a chapter president, and he just laid hands on me. What are you going to do about that?"

"Fuck off, King. Everything he said is true. You didn't need to come all this way. Is it you who betrayed the MC?"

"What?"

"Or did you let your VP fuck you over and turn a blind eye?"

King staggers back. "What are you fucking talking about?"

A knock sounds on the door, and Salvatore Agostino enters the room. "Am I interrupting something?"

"No. I was just asking King about our ventures in Vegas."

"The MC is my life. How can you think I'd betray it?" King's words seem sincere. "Bulldog did this?"

Dane turns, his face a mask of anger as he stares at me. "Sit down." Over his shoulder to King, he says, "You too."

Dane takes his place at the head of the table, and King pulls out a chair and falls into it. All the anger from before is seemingly gone.

Sal sits, his expression one I can't read.

"Sal, perhaps you'd like to tell King all that we

know?" Dane says as he glares at me.

"Thanks to Dirt's dogged determination—"

I cut Sal off, "It wasn't me, it was Guru."

"Yes, but you pointed him in the right direction."

"That's—"

"Dirt, shut the fuck up and let Sal speak," thunders Dane as he slams his hand down on the table.

My lips go into a hard, thin line, and I nod once. My anger is getting the best of me, and I know it's because of the way King spoke about Lore. I put my hands under the table and dig my nails into my hand to keep myself in check.

Sal gives me a tight smile. "As I was saying, we did some digging, and your VP, Bulldog, is having money funneled to him from a woman. Dirt, what is her name?"

"Dee Tremone."

"Deedee," King replies and slumps in the chair. "How much?"

"Does it matter?" asks Sal.

King shakes his head and looks at Dane. "And you think I knew?"

Dane spreads his hands out on the table. "Hopefully, no, but at best, you've run a fucking shoddy chapter." Dane stands and leans over the table. "We had a shooting here, and we sent it out on the wire like we're supposed to, but you've lost members and nothing. Why?"

King rocks back and forth in his seat as he processes all the information. "Because I didn't want to look weak."

Dane scoffs and crosses his arms over his chest.

"No, it's true. We can't all be the great Dane Reynolds who had the money to pull out of drugs and guns and married a fucking rock star."

"You keep my wife out of it."

"Okay, okay, let's talk about the casinos. How? Hmm? How the fuck did you even get in on a deal? For years, all the MCs in Vegas have ever been to the fucking Italians is fodder for their wars. We do their dirty work, then one day you come to town, and suddenly, we are partners in not one but two casinos." By the time he's finished his rant, King is yelling.

Sal makes a noise, and all heads swing in his direction. "You're jealous," he states.

King throws a hand in the air and stares at the wall.

"King, I'm not one of you. When I first came to Tourmaline, my task was to discover why we, the Abruzzi family, were being squeezed out of the gun trade. I was sent in to find out what was going on and, if necessary, neutralize the threat. Instead, I found Dane's sister, who became my wife, and the Savage Angels," he pauses. "I've found Dane to be a man of his word. It's the reason we have a handshake deal. I'm the owner of the casinos, but

I'm part of the Abruzzi family and a captain in their organization. They did not take it well when I went ahead with these deals with Dane. Out of my own profits from the casinos, I pay them a tribute, but I clearly underestimated their desire to have control, just like you've let jealousy cloud your judgment. As a consequence, your VP has allowed the very people we needed to keep out of the casinos in."

King stares at him and then swings his head in Dane's direction. "What are we going to do about Bulldog?"

"Nothing right now," states Dane, but he motions for Sal to keep talking.

"You're going to get our people back in the casinos and be smart, only those with no criminal records. I'm going to position myself in Vegas and oversee the whole operation, including the parts of the business you were in charge of. You're going to tell your men it's a temporary thing and make it sound like I'm giving you a break. As for Bulldog, do nothing. Let him think he's got one over on us. Observe who he's close to, and when the time is right, we will wipe them all out."

Sal's words hang in the air like a weight around our necks. The gravity of his revelation settles in, casting a solemn shadow over the room.

"What about the missing MC members?" King asks.

"When the time is right, we will avenge our fallen

members," states Dane with steel-like resolve.

"And me?"

"Do your fucking job. Inform us when things aren't running like the should or you have a problem. I didn't send out to you and everyone else we'd had a shooting so you'd all come here. I did it as it's how we agreed to operate with open communication. Change has to start with the heads of the MC. Without it, we're fucking lost. Problems, like the shit we're dealing with, spread within our ranks, and I won't tolerate it. Just like I won't have you challenge me in public. Ever. Again."

King takes a deep breath and nods once.

Dane looks at Sal. "Get it done fast, Sal."

"We're working on it," Sal replies.

"Okay, we're done here." Dane strides from the room as do Sal and Jonas, leaving me alone with King.

"He's talking about a war with one of the biggest organizations operating in Vegas," King says, his voice low.

"Yeah. But they've left us no choice."

"You're down with this?"

I stand. My hands are still in fists, my nails digging into my palms. "No matter what, I stand next to Dane. My patch demands that loyalty, but more importantly, so does my soul."

Walking from the room, I don't give King a backward glance, and I keep going until I get to my bike. I cast a glance around the compound I've called home for more years than I care to count and wonder what will become of it and us.

CHAPTER 15

DANE

Dirt strides from the clubhouse, and Sal nudges me to follow him outside. We've both got eyes on Dirt and watch as he takes a look around, shakes his head, and roars out of the compound.

"His head isn't in the game."

Sal nods. "I've never seen him lose his composure like that."

"I have, but it's been a long time." Shaking my head, I lock eyes with Sal. "Lore can push his buttons like no one ever has or will."

"Not even you?"

"Dirt is loyal, and I know he'd take a bullet for me, but if he had to choose between me and Lore? I think he'd choose Lore."

"You can't be serious?"

Raising my eyebrows, I nod. "Ten years ago, they nearly destroyed each other. This time is different. They're older, wiser, and are both searching for the same thing."

"And what's that?"

I laugh. "Each other."

"Dane!" yells Jonas.

"Yeah?" I yell back without turning around.

"Phone call."

"Be there in a sec." Turning, I say to Sal, "The women and our kids need a safe place. Suggestions?"

He nods. "Yes. They all go back with Dave and Luther to Hawaii, along with the band. No one will think anything of it."

"Group vacation?"

"Yes. The only extra person will be Tony."

"I thought Tony stuck with you?" I ask.

"Tony goes where I tell him, and he knows if something were to happen to my family, especially Emily, well, I'd burn the world down. No one would be safe."

Sal smiles, and I'm reminded of how cold and calculating he can be. After all, he didn't become a captain in the Abruzzi Crime Family without killing, torturing, or bribing anyone he needed.

"You going home?"

"Your wife and mine want pie from Howie."

I tap a finger to my lips. "And ice cream

for the kids?"

Sal grins. "Yes."

"Need a ride?"

"No. Tony is at the diner. I'm going to walk there."

Sal gives me a slight tilt of his head and heads into town. He's dressed in one of his black suits with a white shirt. I don't think I've ever seen him in jeans. Maybe once in a T-shirt.

Walking back into the clubhouse, I pick up the telephone on the bar top. "Hello?"

"Dane, Sheriff Morales. Can you come down to the station?"

"Sound official, Carlos."

"It is." Sheriff Morales ends the call.

"*Great.*" I put the telephone back in its cradle and look at Jonas. "You could have told me it was Carlos."

"What did he want?"

"For me to come down to the station."

Jonas gives me a lopsided smile. "I called Destiny. She told me to tell you to pick her up on the way through."

"At least you did one thing right."

Jonas shrugs. "I figured Carlos would be dragging you in. One of the boys gave Izzy a hard time. He might have wrecked one of her ATVs."

"Why am I only hearing about this now?"

Jonas looks at King. "We had other things to

discuss this morning. I was getting to it."

It's going to be one of those days. Walking outside, I get on my Harley and drive the short distance to the law firm where Destiny works. She's waiting outside with a briefcase in hand, wearing a short black skirt and six-inch heels.

Pulling up next to the sidewalk, I hold out my hand. She places her hand in mine and climbs on the back as though she was born to it.

"You should have worn pants."

"Why? I've got great legs."

Laughing, I nod. "Yes, you do. And if you tell Kat or Kade I said that, I'll deny it."

We ride to the end of Main Street in less than a minute. Destiny climbs off and pulls her skirt down. One of the town deputies whistles at her, and she stares at him with no emotion. Slowly, the grin on his face slips, and eventually, his eyes hit the pavement.

I smirk at her, and she arches an eyebrow at me.

Holding open the door to the police station, she walks in first, puts her briefcase on the counter, and says, "I'm Destiny Bennett, and I'm here with my client, Dane Reynolds, to see Sheriff Morales."

"Come on, Destiny, it's me, Frank. I know who you both are."

"Well, Frank, go relay my message to the sheriff."

Frank frowns. "Pretty sure he knows who you both are too."

Chuckling at their banter, I ask, "Are we cool to go and knock on his door, Frank?"

"Go on through. He's expecting you."

I swing open the bullpen gate, and Destiny walks through the station all the way to the back, where Sheriff Morales has his office. She raps on the door twice and then opens it.

"Sheriff Morales, I'm Destiny Bennett, and I'm here with my client, Dane Reynolds."

Carlos is sitting behind his desk. He raises his eyebrows at me.

I hold my hands out wide. "Hey, you're the one who said it was official."

"Shut the door." He points at Destiny. "Does she really need to be here?"

"Yes, Sheriff Morales, I do." Destiny sits and crosses her legs, then looks expectantly at him.

"Carlos, if you called me down here over the ATV thing with Izzy, I'll fix it. I'll even pay for it. There was no need to drag me in here."

Carlos leans forward in his chair and gestures for me to sit, then he clasps his hands together on his desk. "I have no idea what you're talking about."

Destiny glances at me, then asks, "Well, why are we here, then?"

"No, now I want to talk about Izzy and her ATVs."

Izzy is Carlos' girlfriend and runs a business with Cassia, who is engaged to Zeke, one of my men. They hire out ATVs in the summer and snowmobiles in the winter.

"One of the guys wrecked one of her ATVs and maybe gave her a hard time."

Carlos stands. "What's his name?"

I shrug. "Don't know."

"Dane, if this was Kat, what would you do?"

"To paraphrase a friend, I'd burn the world down. But apart from knowing what happened, I don't know who it was. I thought you were bringing me down here to bust my balls over it, so if it's not that, why'd you want to see me, Carlos?"

He stares at Destiny. "Does she need to be here?"

Reaching over, I put my hand on Destiny's shoulder. "Destiny is one of us, and she's a lawyer. I trust her."

He sighs and sits. "Got a call from a friend in the FBI. Seems they are investigating the Abruzzis, and your name came up."

"In what context?" asks Destiny.

"Their wiretap suggests you're on a hit list."

Destiny looks at me, fear in her eyes. "What did you do?"

"Nothing... yet."

Destiny directs her gaze to Carlos. "Why are you telling him this?"

Carlos smiles. "We're friends." Then he locks eyes with me. "And I owe him."

"You know that's the first time you've called me a friend."

Carlos ignores my comment. "We have a deal, Dane, no violence in Tourmaline."

"I can't help it if someone wants to kill me."

"Your lawyer asked a good question. What did you do?"

Standing, I hold out a hand to Destiny and help her to her feet. "Like I told Destiny, nothing yet."

"Why do they want you dead?" Carlos rephrases his question.

"It's the way this business goes sometimes," I reply cryptically.

Carlos rises. "Make sure there's no bad business in Tourmaline."

Holding up a hand to stop him from another sermon, I say, "I know, I know. You don't want any trouble in Tourmaline. It might surprise you to know I don't want anything bad to happen here either."

He holds out his hand, and I shake it. "You call me if you need anything. Got it?"

Grinning, I reply, "We take care of ourselves. See you, Carlos."

I escort Destiny out of the police station, and she lays a hand on my arm. "Is trouble coming?"

Shrugging, I lean against my bike. "We are trying to prevent that from happening."

"We?"

"You've been around us long enough to know that when I say club business, it's the end of the conversation."

"As your lawyer, I expect you to keep me abreast of the situation."

I arch an eyebrow at her and cross my arms over my chest. "Don't forget who I am. I'm not your fiancé."

Destiny looks up and down Main Street and takes a deep breath. "I meant no offense, but..."

"But Kade is in the mix." I uncross my arms. "Trust me when I tell you, we have steps in motion to prevent bloodshed."

"I'm going to walk back to my office. I think I need to clear my head."

She turns and walks away, and I'm left hoping what I've just told her doesn't come back to haunt me.

CHAPTER
16

DIRT

Never did I imagine a second shot with Lore, and yet here she is, as my existence teeters on the brink of collision with the looming threat of a conflict with the Abruzzi clan. Possessing Lore while remaining in the Savage Angels seems like a dream.

I'm outside Tobias' room, about to walk in when I hear a conversation within.

"How are you holding up?" asks Lore.

"I'm hanging in there. Doing what I'm told."

"That's a first." She chuckles then says, "I have no doubt you'll recover, being stubborn runs in our family."

"Yeah, a family trait." There's a pause. "You okay, Mom?"

"You're the one lying in a hospital bed, and

you're asking about me?"

"Can't help it. I'm your son. It's my job to worry about you."

Lore laughs softly. "Ugh, I'm all over the place."

"Whatever it is, Mom, you know you can talk to me about it," he says softly. "I'm here for you, no matter what."

"All right, I've been struggling with my... feelings for Dirt."

This is where a good man would leave a private conversation between mother and son, but I need to know how she feels.

"Being around him is like having a wildfire roaring inside me," she confesses. "But at the same time, I'm terrified."

"Of what?" Tobias asks.

"Of losing him." Lore's voice is barely audible. "The MC lifestyle is dangerous, and I can't help but worry that one day, it'll swallow him whole."

"I get that, Mom. But you know Dirt can handle himself. He's been part of that world for a long time."

"I know," Lore admits. "But that doesn't make it any easier."

"Mom," Tobias says gently. "You can't let fear dictate your decisions. If you love Dirt and want to be with him, you have to trust him to make the right choice."

Knocking on his door as I don't want to hear

anymore, I smile at the two of them. "Hey, man, thought I'd come visit. How you doing?"

Tobias smiles. "I'm doing well. Doc says I can go home soon."

Lore stands, and I kiss her lips, then look at Tobias. "You shouldn't rush it."

"Now you sound like her."

Draping an arm around her shoulders, I say, "Well, your mother is a smart woman."

Lore lightly slaps my stomach. "I don't know about that."

"He's right, Mom, you are, and what's more, you know it." Tobias yawns. "I must be due for a nap."

"Honey, I only just got here." Lore moves away from me.

"Sorry, Mom, I think I overdid it in therapy." His gaze flicks to me. "Dirt, why don't you take her out of here and make sure she gets something to eat?"

"I can do that."

Lore frowns. "I'll be back tomorrow."

Tobias chuckles. "I'll be here."

Lore walks ahead of me out of the room, and I turn to look back at Tobias. "Enjoy your nap."

"Talk to my mother," he says with no small amount of force. "And don't fuck it up."

Gripping Lore's hair around my fist, I pound in and out of her as she whispers my name like a prayer. Her knuckles are white as they grip the vanity in the bathroom of this cheap motel. Burying my face in her neck, I taste the saltiness of her skin with each press of my lips. My hands roam her body, driven by an intense need to touch every square inch of her.

Our bodies slam together, creating a rhythm that echoes through the small space. Each sound we make fuels the inferno between us.

"Please," she begs, her voice desperate and pleading. "Don't stop."

Together, we climb higher and higher, the world beyond fading away until there is only this moment, this connection, and this all-consuming love.

"Come for me," I whisper in her ear, my voice thick with emotion.

And she does. Lore shatters beneath me, the force of her climax ripping through her like a tidal wave as she clings to the vanity for dear life. Moments later, my body tenses with the intensity of my release before we both collapse in a tangled heap of limbs and sweat onto the cold tile floor.

As our breaths steady and the aftershocks of pleasure subside, we lay wrapped in each other's arms, and I want this moment to last forever. Lore's fingers trace circles on my chest as I brush her hair away from her face.

"We're meant to be together, no matter where life takes us."

Lore raises up on one arm. "Dirt—"

I hold a finger to her lips. "What if I take a leave of absence? Say, three months? Lore, I've been in so long, I don't know if I can even function outside the MC, but for you, I'd be willing to try." The words tumble from my lips in a hurried declaration.

"You'd do that for me?"

"Yes. If you'll have me?"

Lore kisses me. "Will Dane do that for you?"

"No fucking idea. It'll go to a vote."

"Six months."

I frown. "What?"

"Three isn't long enough, but six? Six will test us. Hell, it's been a long time since I've shared my life with anyone. You were the last."

"Me too," I confess. "Okay, six months."

"Don't fuck with me on this, Dirt. My heart has had enough scares these past weeks. I'm not sure I could handle another."

Chuckling, I cup her face. "There's my spitfire. I'll ask. Can't promise you anything right now, but I'll ask."

"And if he says no?"

A million thoughts race through my mind.

Would I leave the MC?

Could we make a long-distance relationship work?

Would Lore still want me if I'm in the MC?

Smiling at her, I say, "Let's cross that bridge if and when we come to it."

Leaving the MC—it feels like cutting off a limb, and yet there's no denying the magnetic pull I feel toward Lore. Her eyes are imprinted on my mind, haunting me both day and night.

"Dammit," I mutter under my breath, running a hand through my hair. My loyalty to the Savage Angels MC has never wavered before, but now something inside me urges me to take the leap, to risk everything for her. Just the thought of Lore's warm embrace makes my heart race, and I know he can't ignore it any longer.

With a duffle bag slung over my shoulder, I take a last look around my home. Closing the door to my home, I exhale slowly, my heart pounding in my chest. I know what I need to do—confront Dane, my president, my friend, and tell him I'm leaving the MC for Lore. The thought sends a shiver down my spine, but there is no turning back now.

The ride to the compound takes me less than twenty minutes. I've lived in Tourmaline for the greater part of my life. I have friends, a home, and the MC here. Leaving it feels wrong, but I know Lore couldn't live here with me.

Climbing off my bike, I stride into the clubhouse. The weight of the countless memories hang on these walls—photographs of brothers long gone, trophies from races won, and various mementos from wild nights out.

"Hey, brother," Rebel calls out as I enter the main room.

I nod at him, my mind too occupied with the task at hand to engage in conversation. The familiar sights and sounds envelop me as I walk through the room—the clatter of billiard balls colliding, the smell of cheap whiskey and stale cigarette smoke, and the low rumble of laughter shared between lifelong friends.

"Shit's about to change," I mutter under my breath.

Scanning the room, I search for Dane.

"If you're looking for Dane, he's over in the garage office."

I give Rebel a nod, do an about-face, and walk across the compound. The door is open. I pause for a moment, clenching my fists and steeling myself for the conversation that lies ahead.

Dane sits behind a massive wooden desk, a fortress of organization in the midst of chaos. His long, dark hair is pulled back into a loose ponytail, and his ice-blue eyes are laser-focused on the documents spread out before him.

"Hey, Dane."

Dane looks up, surprise flickering across his face when he sees me. "Dirt, what's going on? You look like you've seen a ghost."

"Uh... w-we need to talk," I stammer, rubbing the back of my neck.

"Sure thing, brother. Have a seat." Dane gestures to the worn leather chair opposite his desk, concern etched into the lines of his face.

"Thanks." I sink heavily into the chair and stare at his hands, callused from years of hard work, as I gather my thoughts. "I don't really know how to say this, so I'm just gonna come out with it."

"All right, shoot. What's on your mind?" Dane leans back in his chair, folding his arms across his chest.

"Look, man... I need to leave the club," I blurt out, then swallow hard, feeling like I've just jumped off a cliff without a parachute.

"Leave the club?" Dane echoes, his voice rising an octave. "What the hell are you talking about?"

"Look, Dane... it's Lore." My voice is barely above

a whisper, as if saying her name aloud makes this decision all the more real. "I can't stay here without her, and she won't stay. You know how she feels about the MC."

"Jesus, Dirt." Dane sighs and runs a hand through his hair. "Permanently?"

"Not to start with. I need six months."

"All right," Dane says finally, his voice heavy with the weight of the moment. "I won't stand in your way, but understand that leaving the club ain't like quitting a job. There could be consequences."

"I know," I reply. "But I've got to do this. For me and for Lore."

"Then go," Dane says quietly. "Just don't forget who you are... and where you came from."

"Thank you, brother." A feeling of relief and bittersweet regret washes over me.

"And if the Abruzzis come for us?"

His question catches me off guard. My immediate thought is, *of course, I'll return,* but if I do, I may lose Lore.

Dane studies me, disappointment in his eyes. "Would you come to stand beside me, brother?"

"Yes."

Dane stands, holds out his hand, and we shake. "May that day never come. See you in six months."

Stepping out of the office and into the sunshine, I inhale a breath and slowly exhale.

Dane let me off easy.

"Hey, Dirt! Where're you headed?" calls out Jonas from a few feet away.

"Got some personal business to take care of," I reply, forcing a smile. "I'll catch you later."

The time for explanations will come, but now is not that moment.

"Take care, man!" Jonas says, raising his hand in a salute.

Striding across the compound, I straddle my bike, turn it on, and rev the engine. With one last look at the clubhouse, I turn my gaze forward and ride away.

CHAPTER
17

DIRT

The morning sun filters through the curtains, casting a warm glow over the bedroom. Lore's soft breathing and the steady rhythm of her heartbeat against my chest are soothing, like a balm to my soul. I breathe in the scent of her hair, cherishing the quiet intimacy of the moment.

As if sensing my wakefulness, Cosmo, her cat, jumps onto the bed, landing squarely on my chest. He turns in a circle a couple of times, kneading his paws into my skin before resting his furry face against my neck.

"Really, Cosmo?" I roll my eyes toward the ceiling, though in truth, I don't mind. Everything I've ever wanted is right here in this bed with me— Lore's warmth pressed against my side, her gentle snores filling my ears, and even her cat purring against my throat.

I miss my brothers in the Savage Angels, but living with Lore and working with her in the bar has brought me a contentment I haven't felt with my brothers in a long time.

My cell phone on the nightstand vibrates, and I reach for it, keeping one arm wrapped tightly around Lore so as not to disturb her slumber.

There's a one-word message, and my heart beats a little faster when I read...

Dane: *WAR*

"Is something wrong?" Lore's sleepy voice interrupts my thoughts, and I quickly lock my phone and set it back down on the nightstand.

"Nothing to worry about," I assure her, though I can feel the weight of the message bearing down on me.

"You're a terrible liar, Dirt," she chides gently, propping herself up on one elbow to look at me. Cosmo rises, meows in her face, and jumps off the bed. "Do they need you?" Lore traces patterns on my chest. "We both know if you wanted back in, Dane would take you."

Covering her hand with my own, I say, "I'm here."

She looks at me, a depth of understanding

passing between us. Lore knows me better than any woman ever has, but beneath the shared affection, there's an unspoken truth—we both know that if I go back to the Savage Angels, I'll lose her forever.

"Good," she murmurs, her voice barely a whisper. "I love you, Dirt."

"I love you too."

The words hold weight, and the sentiment is genuine. Yet, as we lay here, entwined in a moment of shared emotion, the knowledge lingers that my ties to the club mean I'll always carry the weight of worry for my brothers and feel the instinct to check up on them, even when miles away. Just because I love Lore doesn't mean it erases the bonds that have shaped my life.

Rising, I pick up my cell phone, go into the bathroom, and slide the door closed. Taking a deep breath, I call Dane.

"You made me a promise a while back. Will you honor it?"

"Hello, Dane."

"Will you?"

Scrubbing a hand down my face, I say, "My word is my bond. I just need to tidy things up here."

"How will Lore react?"

"We both know she'll handle it badly."

"Make her understand." Dane ends the call.

A soft knock sounds on the door, and I slide it open. Lore is standing there in one of my old black

T-shirts, a sad smile on her face.

"Since when do you make secret phone calls in the bathroom?"

Taking her hand, I lead her back to the bed and sit on the edge of it.

"Dane sent me a text message, and I wanted to talk to him."

"And?" she whispers.

"You know, leaving the MC wasn't easy," I admit, my voice rough with emotion. "Those guys are my family and were my entire world. But, being here, with you... it feels like I'm starting to build something new."

"I feel the same." Lore takes both my hands in hers. "Don't go."

Pulling her closer, I press a tender kiss to her forehead. "I made a promise."

She pulls back. "You made me a promise too."

"I'll come back."

Lore moves away from me, a single tear running down her cheek. "Fine. Go," she chokes out.

"Lore, I love you, but part of who I am was being the sergeant at arms in the Savage Angels, and that hasn't changed. I'm still in. I took a leave of absence, but I didn't quit."

"Y'know, I never thought we'd find our way back to each other, and you could make me feel like this again. But you've proven me wrong, Dirt. You've shown me it's possible to trust and love again, even when we hurt each other so badly before. Don't destroy what we have now by going back."

"I know we've been through a lot, and there's no telling what kind of challenges we might face down the road, but I want you to know that I'm in this for the long haul, Lore. It's just this one last thing, and then I'm out."

"For good?"

"Yes."

The sun dips low on the horizon as I throttle my Harley, the throaty roar of the engine echoing off the buildings as I ride through Tourmaline. Part of me longs for the days when life was simpler, and the open road was all that mattered to my MC brothers and me.

As I approach the clubhouse, the weight of Dane's text and my vow to Lore press heavily on my chest. The tension between the Savage Angels and the Abruzzi Crime Family has reached a boiling point, and war is imminent. Dane wouldn't have called me back if the situation weren't dire—the decision to leave Lore behind in Willowbrook Falls was a difficult one, but loyalty demanded it.

"About damn time you got your ass back here," Dane says as I pull into the compound, his ice-blue eyes narrowing slightly. "You're just in time for the shitstorm."

"Wouldn't miss it for the world, brother," I reply gruffly, swinging my leg over the bike and looking around at the familiar surroundings.

"Things have gotten worse since we last spoke," Dane admits, running a hand through his long, dark hair. "I've sent Kat and kids to Hawaii, under constant guard. Can't risk them getting caught in the crossfire."

"So, what's the plan?"

"Still working on that," Dane sighs, leading Dirt inside the clubhouse. "But we'll figure it out. We always do."

"Damn right, we do," I agree, clapping Dane on the shoulder. This wasn't the first time we'd stared down adversity, and he knew it wouldn't be the last.

As we walked through the dimly lit interior, I couldn't help but feel the crushing weight of responsibility bearing down on me. With the threat of war looming large, is love worth the price of loyalty? Should I have come back?

"Whatever happens, we stick together," Dane says as if reading my thoughts. "We're family, and nothing comes before that."

"Right," I whisper, feeling like a fraud.

"We're flying to Vegas. We need to deal with

Bulldog and meet up with Sal. Jonas is going to stay here and look after things, but I need someone I can trust to have my back." Dane's eyes bore into mine.

"Always, brother. When do we leave?"

"Now."

CHAPTER
18

DANE

The secluded bar on the outskirts of Las Vegas is a far cry from the bright lights and glamour most visitors to the city experience. It is a place where people go when they don't want to be found, where whispers are currency, and secrets can be traded like poker chips.

I pull up in front of the bar, the motorcycle I borrowed from King roaring beneath me as Dirt parks beside me. We dismount our bikes and lock eyes for a brief moment. We both know the stakes are high, and the meeting we are about to have could change everything. Taking a deep breath, I inhale the scent of stale beer and cigarette smoke drifting out from the dimly lit entrance. I've always been good at reading people, and tonight will be no exception.

"Let's do this," Dirt says tersely, adjusting his leather cut as he strides toward the entrance.

As we enter the dingy establishment, we immediately spot Salvatore Agostino sitting alone in a dark corner booth. His slicked-back black hair gleams under the dim lighting while his cold, calculating brown eyes seem to pierce through us.

"Salvatore," I greet him and force a smile to my face as I slide into the booth. "It's been a while."

"Indeed it has, Dane." Salvatore's voice is smooth, almost unnervingly so. "It's good to see you, Dirt. You've been gone for too long."

"Seems I've walked back into a shitstorm."

"Ah, yes, one we'll conquer together," Salvatore says. "Are you glad to be back?"

"Not really," Dirt replies, his muscles tense as he sits next to me.

"Let's cut the pleasantries," I interject. "We're here for a reason."

"Of course," Sal replies, leaning back in his seat and lacing his fingers together on the table.

I glance around the bar, noting the other patrons who seem to be doing their best not to make eye contact. I can feel the tension in the air, thick and suffocating like a noose tightening around their necks.

How the hell did we get ourselves into this?

We are playing a dangerous game, and one false

move could send us and our families plummeting into chaos.

"Very well," Salvatore says, leaning forward and fixing Dane with a piercing gaze. "I'm listening."

Taking a deep breath, I run my fingers through my hair, trying to find the right words. "Your family has been pushing into our territory in Vegas. It's caused problems for both of us. They've disrespected both of us. It's time we strike back."

Sal sighs. "Agreed."

I clench my fists beneath the table, feeling the weight of responsibility on my shoulders. "We've had some... incidents at the casinos. The Abruzzi family has also been trying to muscle in on our strip clubs and tattoo parlors here in Vegas, not to mention Chicago. It's affecting our bottom line, Sal. This is not something we can ignore. We need to come to an understanding."

Salvatore's face remains impassive, betraying no emotion as he considers my words.

"Indeed," Sal replies, steepling his fingers under his chin. "They've overstepped, and we need to strike."

My heart pounds in my chest, and my mind races with the potential consequences of this meeting. Salvatore is a man driven by power and ambition, but he also loves his wife, my sister, Emily. Betraying his own goes against everything he believes in.

Salvatore's gaze never wavers, his eyes burrowing into mine as if searching for any hint of weakness. The silence between us stretches on, and the tension in the air is palpable.

"All right," he says quietly, leaning forward. "Let's talk about how we can resolve this situation."

"Kill the current head of the Abruzzi family," I say, holding Sal's gaze even as the words send a chill down my spine. "With him out of the way, you could step up as the new leader."

For a moment, Salvatore's face betrays no emotion, but then his dark eyes glitter. I can almost see the gears turning in his head as he contemplates the idea.

"My men and I have tossed the idea around," Sal murmurs, his fingers tapping on the table. "The families haven't had conflict like this in a long time. Not all of them will back me."

"Without the current leadership pushing for expansion into our territory, we'd be able to maintain our hold on Las Vegas without further conflict. In return, we'd throw our support behind you as the new head of the Abruzzi family. You'd have a formidable ally in us."

Sal's eyes narrow as he considers the proposal. "And what makes you think I can just step in and take over?" he asks skeptically. "There are protocols, loyalties..."

"I know it won't be easy, but I believe you're the

only man who can hold the families together. You're ambitious, and everyone knows that. We need someone like you in a position of power to help maintain peace between our organizations."

Silence falls over the table as Sal stares at me, weighing the potential benefits and consequences of such a bold move. His fingers drum on the table, and I see the hesitation in his eyes.

"All right," Salvatore says finally, leaning in closer. "I'll consider it. But I need to think this through carefully. If we do this, there's no turning back."

"Understood." I know we are playing a dangerous game, but if it means protecting my MC family and creating a more stable future for both our organizations, I'm willing to take the risk.

Sal's gaze grows distant as he weighs the risks. "There's another problem," he admits, his voice low and measured. "One of the families closest to the Don won't accept me as their leader. They're loyal to a fault, and they'd view my succession as a betrayal."

"So, it could mean more bloodshed?"

"Exactly." Sal frowns, running a hand through his slicked-back hair. "It's not that I'm afraid of a fight, but I don't want to drag innocent people into this mess."

"Neither do I," I agree. "But we can't let the Abruzzi family keep pushing us around. We need to take a stand now, or we'll be crushed under their heels."

"Yes," Sal says, his fingers drumming on the table once more. "But I have to protect those close to me. My wife and kids are safe in Hawaii with yours, but I also have men within my organization who will need protection. If word gets out about our plans, they could be targeted."

"Of course," Dane replies understandingly. "You should do whatever it takes to keep them safe."

"All right," Sal says, meeting my gaze with a steely determination. "If we're going to do this, we need to be smart."

Leaning forward, my eyes lock onto Sal's, and I say, "Let me be clear, we're in this together. We'll protect our families and those closest to us and take down the Abruzzis side by side."

"Together, we'll end their reign and keep those we love out of harm's way." He extends his hand across the table, and I shake it firmly, sealing our alliance.

"I have men loyal to me who are in Don Abruzzi's inner circle. I'll contact them, and we'll put the wheels in motion."

"And I'll clean house here in Vegas. Bulldog needs to be put down."

With that, we exchange a final nod and part ways. I walk out of the bar with Dirt at my side, both of us tense and on high alert.

As we climb onto our motorcycles, I glance over at Dirt, noticing the worry lines etched into his face. It is clear he feels the burden of what we need to do as well.

"Stay sharp, brother," I murmur as we rev our engines. "We've got a long road ahead of us."

"Always," Dirt replies, his brown eyes serious and unwavering. "We'll see this through, no matter what."

With that, we speed off into the night, the path before us uncertain and fraught with danger. But we are united in a purpose, determined to protect our families and bring down the Abruzzis, whatever the cost.

CHAPTER 19

DIRT

As we pull into the Savage Angels compound in Vegas, I sweep my gaze over the building and surrounding area, searching for any signs of danger.

"Keep your guard up, brother," Dane says as we dismount our bikes. "We're playing with fire here."

"Always do," I reply.

We stride toward the entrance, our boots crunching on the gravel beneath us.

"Yo, Dane!" one of the club members calls out from the shadows, his voice slurred. "How'd the meetin' go?"

"Complicated," Dane answers tersely.

Suddenly, a gunshot rings out, echoing through the night like a clap of thunder. The bullet misses both of us and loudly ricochets into the side of the clubhouse, exploding bits of concrete in the air. Time seems to slow as I watch Dane instinctively turn toward the sound, his ice-blue eyes narrowing in on the source. A figure emerges from the shadows, a gun aimed squarely at Dane's chest.

"Look out!" I yell, lunging in front of him as the trigger is pulled.

The bullet tears through my shoulder, and I stagger back. Dane catches me before I can fall, his face a mask of fury.

"Son of a bitch!" Dane roars, pulling out his gun and firing several shots at the assailant. The shadowy figure crumples to the ground, lifeless.

"Stay with me, brother," Dane urges me as blood seeps from my shoulder wound. "We're gonna get you patched up."

"Damn, that hurts," I grit out. "Didn't think I'd take a bullet for you today."

"Can't thank you enough," Dane replies, his voice thick with emotion.

"Next time, *you* can get shot."

Men stream out of the clubhouse, guns drawn.

King is the first to reach us. "What the fuck happened?"

"Someone tried to kill me," answers Dane, looking down at me. "But Dirt took the bullet."

"Who?" asks King.

Dane shakes his head and gestures toward the

prone form on the ground. "The piece of shit over there."

"Help me to my feet, Prez."

King and Dane place a hand under each of my arms, helping me stand. The throbbing pain in my shoulder intensifies, and blood begins to flow more freely down my front.

"King, lead me to your medic."

"You're a tough old bastard, aren't you, Dirt?"

"You have no fucking idea. This happened on *your* watch. Don't think I won't be looking for compensation from your chapter."

His eyebrows go up in surprise, and I glance at Dane, who's smirking.

"He has a point, King."

On my own steam, I walk into the clubhouse. One of the club's girls takes one look at me and points to a door. "Keep walking toward the door in the back. I'll be with you in a minute."

This clubhouse is all tacky carpet and chrome, so different to our home in Tourmaline. When I walk through the door, I'm surprised to see no carpet or chrome. The woman from out front catches up with me.

"What?" she asks.

"It's like night and day."

Smiling, she points to another door. "Yeah, out there is for the tourists... back here is for the Savage Angels." She walks ahead of me and opens the door.

"I'm Katalyst, your friendly medic, and my ol' man is Havoc."

"I'm Dirt. Medic? You ex-army?"

"Guilty as charged."

I sit in a chair. "Me too."

Katalyst opens a drawer and pulls out a pair of scissors.

"You're not cutting anything off me. It's a through and through." Grunting in pain, I slip off my cut and pull my T-shirt over my head with one hand.

She puts the scissors down, puts gloves on, and presses on my wound.

"Fuck me sideways," I say through gritted teeth.

"You're right. It's a through and through. Doesn't feel like you've broken anything." Katalyst's gloved hands work quickly as she applies pressure to the wound.

Antiseptic meets torn flesh, and a hiss escapes me. Katalyst skillfully dresses the wound, the sterile bandage turning crimson as she works.

"I'm going to need you to lie down so I can clean and sew you up." She pulls off her gloves, opens another drawer, and puts a sterile paper cloth over a bed.

With effort, I stand and lay down as she puts on another set of gloves and places everything she needs on a tray.

Katalyst carefully unwraps the dressing from my

shoulder, revealing the ragged entry and exit points of the bullet. Her brow is furrowed, her eyes narrowing in concentration. She reaches for a basin filled with sterile saline solution, the liquid catching the dim light as she moistens a sterile cloth.

"All right, Dirt." Her voice is steady despite the intensity of the situation. "This might sting a bit, but we need to clean the wound."

"I don't want pain relief."

"It's going to sting like a motherfucker."

"Don't care."

With deliberate gentleness, she begins to cleanse the area around the gunshot wound, carefully removing any debris and foreign particles. I wince as the cool liquid touches the raw edges of my torn flesh, a sharp reminder of the violence that has unfolded.

Katalyst's movements are methodical, her gloved hands skilled in navigating the contours of the injury. As the wound becomes free of dirt and contaminants, she studies it with a critical eye. Satisfied with the cleanliness, she reaches for a sterile suture kit, its contents glinting under the harsh lights.

"Now comes the part where we stitch you up," Katalyst explains, giving me a reassuring smile. She threads a needle with precision, the thin strand of suture material gleaming in the light.

With steady hands, she meticulously sutures the

wound, the needle dancing through the torn flesh, each stitch a careful show of skill and experience.

As she nears the end of the suturing process, she tightens the final knot, securing the wound.

"Take it easy for a while, Dirt," Katalyst advises, her tone softens with genuine concern. "We'll get you back on the road soon enough."

"I'm sure you can tell it's not my first rodeo." The scars on my body are a testament to a life well lived.

"Then you know better than to do anything to damage my handiwork."

"Yes, ma'am."

Dane enters the room without knocking. "You okay?"

"No, I caught a bullet."

Dane laughs. "You're fine then?"

"Yes, Prez, I'm fine. Meet Katalyst... she stitched me up good."

Dane nods at her. "Appreciate it."

She shrugs. "Technically, you didn't catch the bullet. It passed right through you."

Katalyst is pulling off her gloves, not an ounce of humor on her face.

"Was that a joke?" I ask.

She smiles. "Yes and no. If you hadn't got shot, we would never have crossed paths."

Dane's forehead furrows in confusion, prompting Katalyst to explain, "It's a twisted kind of fate, Prez. A bullet brings people together in the strangest ways." His frown deepens, but before he can respond, Katalyst continues, "Anyway, Dirt, you should take it easy for a bit. No unnecessary heroics."

"Got it," I respond, giving a half smile. The room settles into a momentary silence, punctuated only by the distant sounds of the clubhouse beyond.

Dane breaks the quiet, his voice carrying a note of seriousness, "We'll need to have a club meeting. Figure out what happened."

Katalyst interjects, "I'll stick around for a bit. Make sure he follows orders."

Dane nods, the weight of responsibility etched on his features.

"Wasn't your fault, Dane," I grunt out as I move into a more comfortable position. "It was the stupid bastard you killed. Who was it?"

"Bulldog."

CHAPTER
20

DANE

The sun dips below the horizon as I stand over Bulldog's lifeless body sprawled on the ground. A pool of blood slowly spreading around his head tells the story of his betrayal and execution.

"Damn traitor," I mutter under my breath, giving the body a disdainful kick. I turn to King, who is standing nearby, just as angry. "We need to find out who else is involved."

King nods, his dark gaze never leaving Bulldog's corpse. "I agree, brother. We can't afford any more..." his voice trails off as he waves a hand over his VP.

Some of the club members move forward to take care of Bulldog's remains. King walks into the clubhouse. We continue through to the back rooms and settle down at the worn wooden table. It is a place where countless decisions have shaped the fate of this MC.

"Who do you think could be next?" King asks, leaning back in his chair and lighting a cigarette.

I rub my chin thoughtfully, my mind racing with possibilities. Every member of the Savage Angels is under suspicion now. Trust is a fragile thing, easily shattered by greed or fear. "I don't know, brother. But we need to find out. Fast."

"Yeah." King exhales a plume of smoke. "But we can't just go accusing people without evidence. That'll cause chaos, and we've got enough problems as it is."

"True. "But we can't let this slide, either. If there's anyone else working with the Abruzzis, they need to be dealt with. Permanently."

King meets my gaze. "You mean..."

"Eliminate them," I confirm, my voice cold and resolute. "It's the only way to protect our club and families."

"Right." King takes a final drag of his cigarette before crushing it in an ashtray. "We'll start digging into everyone's background to see if we can find any connections to the Abruzzis. We've gotta be careful, though. We don't want to tip off anyone who might be guilty."

They have to tread carefully in this dangerous game of loyalty and betrayal. But I can't shake the nagging feeling that time is running out, and more blood will be spilled before this war with the Abruzzi family is over.

Folding my arms across my chest, I say, "Let's get to work. No matter what it takes, we're gonna root out any traitors in our midst and send a clear message that nobody messes with the Savage Angels MC."

I'm sitting in a chair near the bed Dirt is sleeping in. He winces as he shifts into a sitting position. The pain from the gunshot wound must feel like a hot poker. He grits his teeth, swallowing down the groan which threatens to escape his lips.

"Hey, Dane." Dirt struggles to keep his voice steady. "Any news on Bulldog's connections?"

"Nothing concrete yet." I move my chair closer to his bedside. "But we're working on it."

"Good." Dirt takes a shaky breath.

His cell phone rings, and I pick it up. "It's Lore. Do you want to take it?"

"If I don't, she'll keep ringing."

Smiling, I answer the call and hand it over to Dirt. "Hey, babe."

I can't hear her, but he's nodding and smiling.

"Better than ever," Dirt lies smoothly, wincing as he shifts in bed again. "Just out on the road with the guys, taking care of some club business."

He looks at me, and I shake my head as he smiles and nods as though she can see him.

"Hey, don't worry about me," he reassures her, forcing a chuckle. "You know me, always landing on my feet." Dirt glances at me and then says, "Same here, Lore."

I laugh as she's obviously telling him she loves him, and he's uncomfortable saying the words back with me in the room.

"Always," he says before ending the call.

"Want some advice, brother?" Dirt nods at me. "Tell her what happened to you before she finds out. There'll be all kinds of hell to pay if you don't."

A veil of darkness envelops the Las Vegas streets as I stand in the shadows, scanning the area for any signs of movement. The neon lights of the city cast a surreal glow on the scene while the distant hum of engines and murmurs of nightlife serve as the soundtrack to their mission.

"Church went well," King's gravelly voice comes through the earpiece, the connection crackling with static. "They're all in. We're takin' out Shadow and his boys tonight."

"Good," I reply as my heart races with anticipation. We need to strike hard and fast against our enemies to protect the club. A surge of determination courses through me, and I clench my fists at my sides, feeling the cold steel of my gun pressing against my palm.

"Keep it clean and quick, brother," I instruct King, knowing we can't afford to make mistakes or leave loose ends. "We need to send a message... don't fuck with the Savage Angels."

"Roger that, Dane."

King is eager for action but also aware of what is at stake. They have to trust each other implicitly for this to succeed.

As I stalk the streets, following the trail of Shadow, I can't help but think about Dirt lying injured in the makeshift hospital bed. If he hadn't taken the bullet, I might not be here.

The sound of gunfire suddenly erupts in the distance, echoing through the night. Instinctively, I duck behind a nearby car, adrenaline pumping through my veins, and listen intently. King and the Savage Angels are doing their part, taking out the higher members of the rival gang.

I need to find Shadow before it is too late. As I

move cautiously through the dimly lit streets, I feel an overwhelming mix of rage and responsibility. The weight of the club's future rests on my shoulders, a burden I willingly bear for the sake of my brothers.

Finally, I catch sight of Shadow in the glow of a flickering streetlight, his face twisted with anger and fear as he barks orders into his phone. With my heart pounding in my ears, I approach with my gun trained on the rival MC leader.

"Shadow," I call out. "Your time is up."

This is the life they have chosen, and tonight, it will be kill or be killed.

CHAPTER 21

DIRT

Wincing as I pull myself into a sitting position on the bed, the pain in my shoulder is a harsh reminder I need to take it easy. Steeling myself, I put my feet on the floor and stand. I know I shouldn't be out of bed, but there is no way I'm letting Dane go to war without me. So through gritted teeth, I try to ignore the throbbing pain, pick up my gun, and head out into the chaos unfolding in the streets of Vegas.

"Where do you think you're going?" asks Katalyst.

"To the fight. Can I borrow a car?"

"You should be resting." She studies me for a moment and then holds up a set of keys. "It's the black beat-up jeep out front. Try and bring it back in one piece."

"Thanks."

"And don't fuck up my handiwork." Katalyst winks and me. "And be careful."

"Yes, ma'am."

Shadow and his group of misfits have a clubhouse in West Vegas. It's northwest of the Strip and known to be dangerous no matter what time of day or night. I climb into the jeep and drive toward the fight.

"Shit," I mutter as bullets fly between the Savage Angels and the rival gang members on the streets.

"Where's Dane?" I shout over the sound of gunfire, searching for my president amidst the carnage.

"Over there!" King points, his eyes narrow with concentration as he fires off another shot. "He's got Shadow cornered!"

My heart races as I see Dane facing off against Shadow, their guns aimed at each other in a deadly standoff. Moving toward them, I notice one of Shadow's men creeping up behind Dane, a knife glinting in his hand.

"Fuck!" I raise my gun and fire without hesitation. The bullet tears through the would-be attacker's chest, sending him sprawling to the ground. I grin despite the pain that flares through my body with each step.

Shadow, momentarily distracted by his man being shot, makes it easy for Dane to shoot him. I watch as he flies backward, his body hitting the ground, lifeless. Dane stands over him and fires his gun. Shadow's head explodes, bone and brain splattering over the sidewalk. He becomes a force of nature, advancing with mechanical precision, methodically eliminating any rival gang member unfortunate enough to cross his path.

As the Savage Angels continue their assault on the rival gang, Sal and his men are striking at the heart of the Abruzzi Crime Family.

Tonight, we will either win or die trying.

The last of Shadow's men were brought down. Las Vegas is painted in red, and the Savage Angels MC has made its mark. But it isn't over yet. We're in the clubhouse, where Dane is anxiously waiting for a call from Sal.

Unable to sit still any longer, Dane pulls his phone out of his pocket and walks outside. I follow him since no one is killing my president tonight.

"Sal, it's Dane. Things have escalated," his voice rough with exhaustion. "Now's the time to strike at the heart of the Abruzzi family We've done our part. It's time for you to do yours." Dane ends the call and looks at me. "Message bank."

"Shit."

"Yeah."

"You worried?"

Dane slips his cell phone back in his pocket. "Yes." He shakes his head and then asks. "I don't like this. Can you travel?"

"Yes, it's a through and through. I'm sore, but I'll be fine."

"Let's get back to Tourmaline."

"Are all the loose ends tied up here?" I ask.

Dane nods once. "All the rats in the clubhouse were weeded out tonight. My only concern is whether Sal and his men struck at the heart of the Abruzzi family. If they haven't, we're in for a world of pain."

"And he's not answering his phone?"

Dane gives a somber shake of his head. "No."

"Shit." I take a deep breath. "Brother, have you called Kat or your sister? Are they safe?"

Dane's steely expression hardens further. The gravity of the unspoken answer hangs heavy in the air. He finally breaks the silence, his voice tight with concern. "Kat's not picking up, and I can't reach my sister. Something's not right."

An uneasy chill settles over me. The air crackles with unspoken fears. Without another word, we both reach for our phones. The weight of unanswered questions threatens to engulf us all.

He nearly lost Kat once and went mad with grief, but to lose her, his sister, and his children?

No one will be left alive.

TO BE CONTINUED

IN

Savage Angels

Kathleen Kelly

If you liked this story,
you can continue with
other books by Kathleen Kelly.

The MacKenny Brothers Series
An MC/Band of Brothers Romance
Spark Book 1
Spark of Vengeance Book 2
Spark of Hope Book 3
Spark of Deception Book 4
Spark of Time Book 5
Spark of Redemption Book 6

Tackling Romance Series
A Sports Romance
Tackling Love Book 1
Tackling Life Book 2

Standalones
Wraith
Cardinal: The Affinity Chronicles Book One
Crude Possession: Crude Souls MC
Snake's Revenge: Gritty Devils MC

The Savage Angels MC Series
Motorcycle Club Romance
Savage Stalker Book 1
Savage Fire Book 2
Savage Town Book 3
Savage Lover Book 4
Savage Sacrifice Book 5
Savage Rebel (Novella) Book 6
Savage Lies Book 7
Savage Life Book 8
Savage Christmas (Novella) Book 9
Savage Release Book 10
Savage Heart Book 11
Savage Angels Book 12

Royal Bastards MC Jacksonville, FL

Creed Book 1
Reaper Book 2
Highway Book 3

CONNECT WITH ME ONLINE

Check these links for more books from
Author Kathleen Kelly

READER GROUP

Want access to fun, prizes and sneak peeks?
Join my Facebook Reader Group.
https://bit.ly/32X17pv

NEWSLETTER

Want to see what's next?
Sign up for my Newsletter.
https://www.subscribepage.com/kathleenkellyauthor

BOOKBUB

Connect with me on Bookbub.
https://www.bookbub.com/authors/kathleen-kelly

GOODREADS

Add my books to your TBR list
on my Goodreads profile.
http://bit.ly/1xsOGxk

AMAZON

Buy my books from my Amazon profile.
https://amzn.to/2JCUT6q

WEBSITE

https://kathleenkellyauthor.com/

TIKTOK

https://www.tiktok.com/@kathleenkellyauthor

TWITTER

https://twitter.com/kkellyauthor

INSTAGRAM

https://instagram.com/kathleenkellyauthor

EMAIL

kathleenkellyauthor@gmail.com

FACEBOOK

https://bit.ly/36jlaQV

ABOUT THE AUTHOR

Kathleen Kelly was born in Penrith, NSW, Australia. When she was four, her family moved to Brisbane, QLD, Australia. Although born in NSW, she considers herself a QUEENSLANDER!

She married her childhood sweetheart, and they live in Toowoomba.

Kathleen enjoys writing contemporary romance novels with a little bit of steam. She draws her inspiration from family, friends, and the people around her. She can often be found in cafes writing and observing the locals.

If you have any questions about her novels or would like to ask Kathleen a question, she can be contacted via e-mail:

kathleenkellyauthor@gmail.com

or she can be found on Facebook. She loves to be contacted by those who love her books.

www.ingramcontent.com/pod-product-compliance
Lightning Source LLC
Chambersburg PA
CBHW051338020726
47501CB00007B/2149